# Now or Never

TOMMY HAMBLEDON is back, and again he's in Germany, posing as a camera-toting tourist while trailing renascent Fascists. The investigation started in Cologne when a corpse was found hung out like a batch of wash from the bare girder of a ruined building.

Then Tommy learned about two quaint girls whose custom it was "to frolic among the ruins" late at night, and found that his buddies, Forgan and Campbell, were on hand to help him unravel the mystery of the Silver Ghosts, the Nazi outfit he was after. Their part was to find the next meeting place of the Ghosts.

After another man had died among the wrecked buildings, the long-awaited message arrived, and the Ghosts were soon to meet for the last time. Then Hambledon and his cohorts discovered the identity of the man who left his fingerprints on an umbrella —and blew the top off an intrigue that might have turned all Europe topsy-turvy.

German scene.
*This novel has not appeared in any form prior to book publication.*

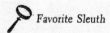 *Favorite Sleuth*

# MANNING COLES

# Now or Never

Doubleday & Company, Inc.
Garden City, New York

*All of the characters in this book are fictitious,*
*and any resemblance to actual persons,*
*living or dead,*
*is purely coincidental.*

# Contents

# Now or Never

# *1  YESTERDAY'S HAPPY MAN*

The moon crept across the sky until its light fell upon
the girder which had a rope on the end of it and on the
rope the body of a man hanging by the neck and turning
slowly, first one way and then the other. From it there
drifted on the night air, faint but unmistakable, the in-
congruous smell of bananas.

Cologne in 1950 is a city of ruins. If a man comes out
from the railway station he will find the Cathedral standing
with its twin towers apparently undamaged, the Excelsior
Hotel looks the same as ever apart from scars from bomb
fragments, and the Dom Hotel, on the opposite side of the
square, still has sixty bedrooms left out of six hundred. The
fourth side of the square, opposite the Cathedral, is all
ruins. If a man crosses the square and walks up what is still
called the Hohestrasse he will find small one-story shops
hastily built of rough brickwork, poured concrete, or timber; over their heads loom the skeletons of tall houses,
roofless, with sagging floors and bent and twisted iron
girders sticking out at all angles like the arms of demented
gallows.

Behind these ruins, on both sides of the Hohestrasse, con-

13

ditions are even worse. Here and there a corner of a building still stands, but in the main there is nothing left but shapeless heaps of rubble of varying heights all overgrown with weeds. Young trees have taken root; some of them after eight years are quite tall with leaves rustling in the wind and birds singing in the branches. Small animals run about in the undergrowth; the country has crept in upon Cologne.

The street called the Grosse Budengasse leads from the Hohestrasse towards the river. Since it was once an important thoroughfare, the surface of the road has been cleared of rubble so that it is possible to pass along it. There is, in one place, a piece of wall left standing about three feet high and just wide enough to permit the authorities to paint the name of the street upon it, though even that is crumbling, so that part of the *B* of Budengasse is now missing.

Four men came along this street pushing a truck loaded with bananas. It was late at night, well after midnight, very late for Cologne, which nowadays goes to bed early, but the moon, past its full, was rising and they could see their way well enough. The four men were all pushing the truck, but bananas are, of course, a heavy fruit. They were stacked in a long heap the whole length of the truck.

"If he hadn't been a fool," said one man in a low tone, "he might have been having his usual instead of this."

"If he'd stuck to beer," said another, "but he would mix it with Steinhager. Serve him right."

"All the same," said a third man, "I don't want another session like we had tonight. A full meeting, and *that* being done in front of us all. I've seen some things, but that——"

"Going to dream about it?"

14

"I hope not, but I shan't forget it in a hurry."

"Of course," said the first man, "that was why the president did it. I reckon any member will think twice before he gets drunk and babbles like that. It's our lives, isn't it?"

"There's a lot more hangs on this than just our lives," said the second man. "By the way, did you see his farewell letter? Oh, you missed something; it was good. Give you my word, if he'd lived long enough to see it he'd have thought he wrote it himself. Gerhardt is clever, isn't he?"

"I wouldn't lend him my chequebook," agreed the first man.

"What did they do with it? Post it?"

"Of course not. It's in his pocket, naturally."

They came to the corner of the Unter Goldschmied and turned right; the road began to rise here and the surface was rough and potholed. The four men bent to their work and the banana truck rumbled on. Not far ahead of them there was a heap of rubble rather larger than usual; a wall, with the iron girders which had supported a floor still sticking out of it, had turned right over so that the end of one girder overhung the path. Bushes had grown thickly on the top of the pile, casting a dark shadow; as the men looked towards it the figure of a girl came into sight and went back again. One of the men pushing the truck checked suddenly, but the leader reassured him. "It's all right, it's only Magda."

When the truck reached the patch of shadow it stopped. Two men and two girls came forward to meet it; the men stayed, but the girls ran past it and parted, one going south towards Laurenzplatz, the other north, the way the truck had come; fifty yards along the road they stood and waited.

There was no suggestion of lounging in their attitude but rather an alertness as of one who is keeping watch.

It was impossible to see in detail what was happening in the shadow; there was only a general impression of activity, as though the bananas were being off-loaded and replaced. Presently the truck came out along the road again, briskly pushed by two men only. It still had bananas upon it, but one would have said that the long mound was not so high as it had been.

A little later the road was quite empty; the girls had disappeared and there was no sign of the four men who had been so busy in the shadows. The moon rose and crossed the sky until that which had been obscure was illuminated. The girder which overhung the path was no longer useless and bare; it had a rope on the end of it and on the rope the body of a man hanging by the neck and turning slowly, first one way and then the other.

Tommy Hambledon was staying at the Gürzenich Hotel which, for reasons of his own, he preferred to the Dom Hotel for this visit. The Gürzenich Hotel, largely destroyed and now partially rebuilt, stands on an island site at the far end of the Unter Goldschmied from the Dom, though one would not take that way from choice because it is now so uncomfortably rough. It still remains a short cut for people coming on foot; the chambermaid on Hambledon's floor came that way every morning just before six from her home between the station and the river.

Hambledon was called later than usual on the following morning; Elsa came into his room so obviously bursting with news that he sat up in bed and looked at her.

"The gracious Herr will forgive my lateness, I beg his

16

pardon," she babbled, "I'm so upset, I saw something—oh dear!"

"Calm yourself," said Hambledon. "I don't mind being called late for once. What is the matter?"

"In the Unter Goldschmied—I come that way—there was a policeman and when I came to him he said, 'Go by quickly, do not look,' so of course I looked and oh, mein Herr, there was a man hanging by a rope from a girder—oh!"

"Only one?" said Tommy.

The girl gaped at him.

"Only one—how many did the Herr expect?"

"None at all. But it would have been a lot worse if there had been a row of them, wouldn't it?"

"Ach!" gasped Elsa, and hurried out of the room.

"I'm afraid I've horrified the poor girl," said Hambledon to himself, "but at least I stopped her describing it to me before breakfast." He threw back the bedclothes and got up. Suicides are not uncommon in a country which has been defeated, although this man seemed to have left it rather late, as it were. Despair comes upon people in the hour of defeat, not, as a rule, five years later. This man, Hambledon assumed, must have had some private reason for doing it. Tommy dismissed the subject from his mind, breakfasted, and strolled down the Hohestrasse in the morning sunlight. He was dressed in tweeds, wearing an English hat and carrying a camera slung from his shoulder; he looked about him as he went, stopping every now and again when anything interested him, the very picture of a harmless tourist.

He reached the Dom Square and wandered about for

some time, watching the people and taking photographs of the Cathedral. He was, actually, waiting in the hope of seeing two friends of his come out of the Dom Hotel; they should have arrived there on the previous day, but when he telephoned the hotel the evening before he was told that the Herren Campbell and Forgan were not yet there. They might come by the late train; their rooms were booked.

Hambledon was approached by an elderly man with a camera, desiring to take his photograph with the Cathedral in the background. The man was one of Cologne's official photographers licensed by the city authorities; he wore an arm band to that effect. Tommy agreed at once and paid six marks for three copies to be delivered at the Gürzenich Hotel the following morning. He entered into conversation with the man, who was very ready to talk since business was anything but brisk.

"It is the rate of exchange," said the photographer. "It is too high, eleven point eight marks to the pound sterling. It keeps the tourists away, and who can wonder? No one is rich in these days. If the exchange went down to twenty or twenty-four to the pound as it used to be, the tourists would come again and a man like me could earn an honest living."

Hambledon looked across at the ruins and wondered what tourists would come to Cologne for, but naturally did not say so. He agreed, and added that a situation already difficult was made more so by the incomprehensible rules of the currency controls on all frontiers. "The customs are bad enough," he said, "but there have always been customs. This currency business——" He shook his head and the photographer sympathized. "You English," he said,

18

"for it is evident that the Herr is English, everyone knows you are severely dealt with by your government in the matter of money."

"Not only my government," said Tommy gloomily. "They all do it except the Americans."

"Ah," said the photographer. "Except the Americans."

"But," said Hambledon, "surely you have numerous German visitors who come to see how their famous city has fared?"

"Groups of children pay best. One photograph, and each of them buys a copy. One can then reduce the price, the Herr understands. But there are not enough of them, and sometimes one has losses. Only yesterday I lost six marks."

Hambledon turned casually so as to face the Dom Hotel and said: "Really? What hard luck. How was that?"

"I took a young man's photograph. I knew him, his father is a manufacturer and well-to-do. He came to me and insisted that I take his photograph in front of the Dom as I have just taken the Herr's. He was a little drunk, not very, just happy and rather unsteady. It was not a very good photograph because he could not stand quite still, the Herr understands. Here it is," said the photographer, pulling an envelope out of his pocket and showing Hambledon a print of a young man with a fair, rather silly face. "He did not pay, but I was not anxious since I knew him. This morning I take the photographs to his house and find it a house of sorrow. He has hanged himself during the night."

"Good gracious," said Hambledon in a shocked voice, "what a dreadful thing."

"So I did not get paid. You understand, one cannot trouble the family about a trifle at such a moment. I apologized and came away quickly. Yet he was happy yesterday; it is strange, is it not? He left me and went across to that *Bierkeller* on the corner there. I saw him go in."

"Drowning his sorrows, perhaps," began Hambledon, but the photographer saw a group of people who were quite obviously visitors and excused himself hastily. There was still no sign of Forgan and Campbell. Hambledon felt that if he stood about much longer he would become conspicuous. He walked away; for want of a more definite errand he went down the Unter Goldschmied to see where yesterday's happy man had hanged himself.

There was no mistaking the spot; there was only one place along that devastated road where a man could find anything high enough to hang himself on. Besides, there was another man already there looking up at the projecting girder, a small square man with a shock of white hair which blew about in the wind. He stood with his legs wide apart and a long shabby waterproof flapping round them, looking keenly at every detail of the scene before him. Hambledon came along and stopped, and the man looked round at him.

"Excuse me," said Tommy. "This is, I take it, the place where that unhappy young man committed suicide last night?"

"This is, indeed, the place."

Hambledon looked at it from several viewpoints.

"The Herr is a visitor?" said the man.

"I am," said Tommy.

"An English visitor."

"The Herr is right again. I am interested in this because the chambermaid at my hotel on her way to work this morning saw the poor young man hanging. It upset her very much."

"It would," said the white-haired man, "it would, naturally. She did not see the other one also?"

"What other one?"

"The other man who hung himself upon this very girder about three months ago."

"How very odd," said Hambledon. "No, she didn't mention it."

"It is odd, as the Herr says. I do not know so many details about the previous suicide as I do about this one; I was not engaged upon the earlier case, but this one has some peculiar features about it."

"The Herr is a detective?"

"A private investigator," said the man. He stepped down from the bank upon which he was standing and gave Hambledon a card from his wallet. It read: "Heinrich Spelmann. Private investigator. Enquiries undertaken with discretion and despatch."

"I see," said Tommy. "No connection with the police."

"None. Absolutely none. The police are no help to me at all, quite the contrary. They have a tendency to tell me to go away. Our poor police, they do their best, but what are they? Young ex-servicemen enrolled for the purpose of keeping order and quite untrained in the finer points of crime investigation. Traffic cops, that is all. The earlier police had to be disbanded—they were politically tainted, the Herr will understand—but with them went all their skill and experience. These poor young men." He shook his head, and his white hair flew out like a halo.

"It must be an exasperation to a man of experience like yourself," said Hambledon.

"It is, it is. Now, in this case, I knew quite a lot about the young gentleman beforehand." Spelmann paused and looked at Hambledon. "The Herr is a visitor and, it is evident, a man of intelligence and probity. He is here now and will presently go home again, he is independent, he is impartial. Let me lay the case before the Herr. It will help to clear my mind."

"Carry on," said Tommy. "Have a cigarette."

"I thank the Herr. I have been engaged by the family of the late Karl Torgius to look into this painful affair and I had an opportunity this morning to examine the body. He did not break his neck; he strangled himself. Now, I have seen many suicides, mein Herr, during these late unhappy years. A man puts a rope round a beam or some similar"—he gestured toward the girder with a curious fluttering of the fingers—"he stands on a chair, or a wall as in this case, puts the noose round his neck, and jumps into space. If he is lucky and the noose is correctly adjusted, he breaks his neck and it is all over. If not, he strangles, a comparatively slow process, and when it begins he invariably— but, invariably, mein Herr—changes his mind. He does not wish to die like that. He grasps the rope with frantic hands, he tries to ease the pressure, he struggles, he tears the skin of his hands. I have seen it so often. But young Karl Torgius hangs there like a rag doll, quite limp, with his arms straight down and his hands less abraded than mine are with scrambling about on this infernal rubble."

"I suppose he did jump from that lump of wall?"

"Undoubtedly. Here are the marks where his feet scraped off the dust."

"It is odd," said Hambledon. "I was talking this morning to a photographer in the Dom Square who took young Torgius' photograph yesterday. He said that the young man was quite happy then, very happy and a little drunk. After that he went across to the Muserkeller at the corner; do you know it?"

"I do, yes."

"Scrambling about in brick dust is thirsty work, Herr Spelmann. Will you do me the honour to have a glass of beer with me? I suggest the Muserkeller."

Spelmann bowed. "I accept with pleasure. Also, since the Muserkeller was one of the places which our poor young friend visited yesterday, I ought to go there. I am obliged to the Herr—the Herr——"

"Hambledon."

"The Herr Hambledon—thank you—for the suggestion. Some hint may await me there which will lead to some explanation of this affair."

They walked along the road together, walking carefully and avoiding the rougher places where bomb holes had simply been filled in with rubble unacquainted with any road roller.

"It is quite plain," said Hambledon, "that you are not satisfied in your mind about this suicide."

"I have not only to satisfy myself," said Spelmann, "I have to satisfy his parents. They consulted me some little time ago; they were uneasy about their son. He was once open and frank in all his doings; he became secretive. He was a home lover; he took to going out late at night and became evasive when asked about it. They suspected that he was having an affair with a lady, and since he did not produce her, it followed that the lady was such as they would not approve. I took some pains to observe his doings, but I was not, unfortunately, successful. I followed him several times at night. He used to come along the Hohestrasse and turn towards this district, where I invariably lost him. I ask the Herr, what is there for a young man in this area of desolation?" Spelmann stopped as they reached the Grosse Budengasse and gestured at the scene. "Brickbats, weeds, and rats. There are also some miserable girls who frolic among the ruins. I thought that he might have become interested in one of them, but I satisfied myself that that was not so."

"Where did he go, then?"

"I have no idea. He used to disappear somewhere about here. I have searched the area by daylight and found nothing. There are cellars under all this debris. I looked into such of them as are accessible and not too unsafe. They are dark, damp, dirty, and malodorous, eerie also, a haunted feeling. There are many thousand dead under those rubble heaps, Herr Hambledon, no one knows how many. Twenty thousand, they say, died in one night in Cologne. Nobody strolls here at night for pleasure."

"I believe you," said Hambledon with emphasis.

"Let us go on; even in daylight this place depresses me. My Köln, mein Herr, my Köln!"

"Reverting to young Torgius," said Hambledon, leading the way towards the Hohestrasse at a smart pace, "has a doctor examined the body?"

"Certainly, yes. It was he who confirmed my opinion that the neck was not broken. Why?"

"I let my imagination run ahead of sense," said Tommy apologetically. "It was your saying that he had not struggled. I wondered whether, perhaps, he had been doped."

"A post-mortem," murmured Spelmann.

"Is there to be one?"

"There will be if I have any say in the matter. The Herr's thoughts run on the same lines as my own."

"I noticed that my suggestion didn't surprise you. Is there much dope-taking in Cologne now?"

"There is some, where is there not? Not much, we have not the money."

"But the Torgius family are well-to-do, you said. I wondered—probably the idea is foolish—I pictured a party of dope-takers and young Torgius passes right out. The others think he is dead; they also are in a stupid state. To cover themselves, they stage a suicide by hanging."

"But he did die by strangulation," said Spelmann.

"Just so. I said that they also were half stupefied. He was not dead then."

Spelmann looked at Hambledon. "The Herr has an ingenious mind. The suggestion is possible."

"So are half a dozen others," said Tommy.

## 2 *MONSIEUR ALBERT BAPTISTE*

The Muserkeller was not a large place, one long room with chairs arranged round small tables and a bar down one side with beer barrels behind it. The bartender, the *Kellner*, was a short man with the traditional blue apron tied round an enormous paunch. Hambledon looked at him and remembered him vaguely from the days of the First World War. The *Kellner* had been a slim young man then; if that was what beer did to you . . .

Hambledon and Spelmann sat down at a table near the door, and the fat man came at once with a glass of beer in each hand, not waiting for an order, and set them on the table. The door of the Dom Hotel was within view, which was the main reason why Tommy had suggested this place. There was still no sign of two familiar figures: one short and stout, the other lean and tall with flaming red hair. Nor of two other men whom Hambledon had never seen but who had been described to him in some detail, dark sallow men, typically Spanish. He decided that as soon as he could get rid of Spelmann he would ring up the Dom Hotel again.

They emptied their glasses since the day was hot, and Cologne is a dusty place in these days; immediately the fat *Kellner* waddled forward with two fresh glasses to replace the first. He would keep this up, Hambledon remembered, until one offered to pay. There were several other men at the other tables; it was not a place to which women went.

Presently another man strolled in who was, it appeared, a friend of Spelmann's. They greeted each other; the man was introduced as Herr Sahl and sat down at their table. He took a packet of Gold Dollar cigarettes from his pocket and opened the top; Hambledon idly watched to see him tear the packet down and scrabble to get out a cigarette, as one usually does with a paper packet. Not at all. Sahl held the packet loosely in one hand and flicked the bottom sharply with one fingernail, whereupon a cigarette obligingly jumped out at the top. Very neat. Hambledon noticed later that Cologne people usually dealt in this way with paper cigarette packets, though whether it was an exclusively local custom he never discovered. He adopted it himself and it always worked.

"Sad about young Torgius," said Sahl.

Spelmann agreed. "I hear he was in here yesterday."

"That's true. I was here at the time. He was—you know —a bit lit. But quite happy. Rather overflowing, in fact. Talking nineteen to the dozen."

Hambledon sat back in his chair and sipped his beer. He felt he had had nearly enough of young Torgius for one morning and he was not really interested.

"Talking a lot of nonsense, I suppose," said Spelmann. "He was rather given that way, God rest his soul."

"Talking about high hopes for a new Germany. Something was going to be done before it was too late, then everybody would see that Germany wasn't finished. He was very pleased about it."

27

"After which he goes off and hangs himself," said Spelmann.

"He did have one morbid moment," said Sahl. "You know how they swing from one extreme to the other——"

"Excuse me," said Spelmann, "but would you mind not using the word 'swing' this morning? I've just seen him. What did he say?"

"Something rather odd, considering all things. He turned quiet all of a sudden, just sat and stared like an owl. Somebody asked him if anything was the matter and he said—listen to this—he said: 'I've seen a hanging. I saw a man hanged. Never want to see that again, never.' Then he had another drink and cheered up again."

"Nobody asked him about it, I suppose?"

"Of course not. Nobody wanted to hear about it, anyway. Well, I suppose he got more morbid as the evening went on and eventually the force of example was too much for him."

"Poor boy," said Spelmann, "poor silly, unbalanced boy."

Hambledon looked again at the Dom Hotel and saw two men come out of the doorway. One wore a wide black hat and a cloak; the clothes of the other, if less exotic, were of unmistakably foreign cut, and yet there was something very familiar about their appearance. They stopped outside the door and looked about them.

Hambledon looked at his watch, uttered an exclamation, and said he would have to go. He paid the rotund *Kellner*, hoped he would meet Spelmann again very soon, and walked off after the men from the Dom Hotel. They went across to an open-air café in the square and sat down at a table; when Hambledon came up to them they rose to their feet and bowed ceremoniously.

"We saw you sitting in that pub," said Forgan.

"We thought you would probably track us down," said Campbell.

"I am very glad indeed to see you," said Hambledon. "Have the Spaniards also arrived?"

"We are the Spaniards," they said with simple dignity.

In the Clerkenwell Road, London, there is a small shop of which the frontage consists only of one window with a door beside it. The window is full of models of all kinds, ships of many types and dates, from the big racing Bermuda-rigged cutter to tiny waterline models of warships. There are miniature railway engines of many types and various methods of propulsion, rolling-stock, permanent-way fittings, spare parts in great variety, and construction sets in cardboard boxes with optimistic pictures on the lids. Over and above all, there is a large wooden model of a barque, fully rigged but without sails and obviously antique. This serves much the same purpose as the great coloured jars in the windows of old-fashioned chemists; it decorates the premises and announces the nature of the business. Neither of the partners would sell it for any money.

The partners were William Forgan, a short, stout man with dark wiry hair going thin on the top, and his friend, Alexander Campbell, a tall red-haired man as lean and stringy as his partner was stout. They had spent many years together as engineers on a ranch in the Argentine; they started this shop when they came home, and it had so prospered that now they employed an elderly assistant of terrifying respectability and an imp of a boy called Jim.

The modelmakers were old friends of Hambledon's and had even worked with him upon occasion.

One evening about three weeks before Karl Torgius died in Cologne, Campbell returned just before closing time from an afternoon spent overhauling an electric railway which was a millionaire shipowner's pride and joy. He found his partner Forgan trying to count up the contents of the till and making rather a mess of it because his mind was not upon what he was doing.

"Twenty-seven, twenty-eight, twenty-nine—how did you get on, Campbell?"

"The set wanted rewiring all through. I did it. That's all."

"Eleven, twelve, thirteen ten-bobs is seven pound ten."

"Six pound ten," corrected Campbell. "Anything happened?"

"Pity you were out. I've had a visitor."

"Really. Who?"

"Hambledon."

"Oh, indeed. Good. What had he to say for himself?"

Forgan looked up at the clock and called to his assistants, who were behind a partition which ran across the back of the shop to screen off workbenches and some small machines.

"Mitchell. Jim. You can pack up now, it's close on six."

The boy Jim put his tools away, the respectable Mr. Mitchell put on his bowler hat and picked up his umbrella; they said good night to the partners and walked out together. Forgan locked the shop door while Campbell pulled down the blind over the window.

"Well?" said Campbell.

"Hambledon's going to Germany, to Cologne, to be

exact. Apparently the Germans have started a new secret society and he is going out to get it."

"Must be something if they're sending out Hambledon."

"He didn't say much about it except that people who try to find out anything are liable to be bumped off. That's why they think it must be important. The trouble is that practically nothing is known about it, who belongs to it or where they meet, except a strong suspicion that the centre's in Cologne."

"Well?" said Campbell again.

"The only thing which is definitely known is that two Spaniards are going from Madrid to meet the organizers in Cologne. Hambledon said that if somebody hung on behind the Spaniards without being unduly noticed, some lead to their German playfellows might be discovered."

"And at that point he thought of us."

"Exactly. All expenses paid and every facility afforded."

"What did you say?"

"That I'd consult you, naturally."

Campbell grinned. "Who are these Spaniards?"

"Alfonso d'Almeida and Miguel Piccione, both of Madrid. They are men in their early forties and members of the Falangista. They are disguised as fruit importers selling oranges to the vitamin-starved countries of Europe."

"And when are they due in Cologne?"

"On Sunday, June the eleventh, three weeks next Sunday. They are going via Paris, where they will spend five days, staying at the Ambassador. They get to Paris on June sixth. In Cologne they will be staying at the Dom Hotel, so Hambledon will be staying at the Hotel Gürzenich for greater freedom of action."

Campbell took a turn up and down the darkened shop, lit only by the daylight filtering through the blinds. Forgan leaned on the counter and watched him.

"Do this society—whatever its name is——"

"The Silver Ghosts," said Forgan.

"Sounds like lepers. Do they and the Spaniards know each other personally?"

Forgan laughed aloud. "Believe it or not, I asked him that. No, they don't. The previous go-between died."

"Then how do they recognize each other?"

"D'Almeida and Piccione are to go to the Dom and just wait there until somebody comes to see them."

"I see. To Be Left Until Called For. Can these Spaniards speak German?"

"Not very well, Hambledon says. They can get along in it."

"Finally—for the moment—why are they going?"

"Apparently it's a Nazi revival. Some of the extreme Fascists in Spain are financing them, or contributing, anyway. D'Almeida and Piccione will be kindly welcomed, don't you think?"

Campbell grinned again. "We didn't have a holiday last year, did we, Forgan?"

"No, we didn't. Mitchell was new then and we felt we couldn't leave him. On the principle that a change of work is a rest, we redecorated the bathroom and kitchen. We came to the conclusion that the saying I quoted is a fallacy. Why?"

"It's a long time since we saw Paris," said Campbell.

"Too long. I had already come to that conclusion myself. If the British Government is going to pay for our stay in

32

Germany, there's nothing to stop us from going to Paris on our holiday allowance first."

"Fifty pounds each. We shouldn't last long at the Ambassador on that."

"Then we must either stay somewhere else or not go across too soon," said Forgan. "I wonder whether Messrs. d'Almeida and Piccione play poker."

"We might teach them," said Campbell, passing through the shop to lock the back door. "It is a simple game and soon learned even by persons of the most moderate intelligence. All ready? Let's go upstairs."

"But we must remember that if we want these Spaniards to cling round our necks in Cologne we mustn't skin them in Paris."

"Well, we needn't overdo it," said Campbell. "Did you gather any idea of how long Hambledon will want us to stay in Germany?"

"Not a hint; I don't suppose he knew himself. Are you thinking about this business?"

"Well, it's our bread and butter," said Campbell apologetically. "Although I suppose if we're out there some time there'll be nothing to stop us from running back here occasionally to see how things are going on. The government won't want us to beggar ourselves for them; they might have to compensate us."

"Don't be so mercenary. Will you make the tea or shall I?"

Monsieur Albert Baptiste was a prosperous-looking little gentleman in very good clothes with an expensive watch chain across his semi-lunar front. He had charming and friendly manners, trustful brown eyes, and an air of unworldly inexperience. He was a confidence trickster by profession; on a previous visit to Paris, Campbell and Forgan had met him in a café where he had practised his art upon them. They had cheerfully allowed themselves to be led along to the point where the climax was imminent and then engaged in an animated discussion with each other, Baptiste being present, about the various ways in which he could arrange the finish. Baptiste listened at first with horror, then with admiration, and finally with gales of laughter which set the tears running down his cheeks.

"Messieurs," he gasped, "have pity. It is quite evident that I, a poor minnow, have challenged a pair of tritons. May I have the honour of knowing where you gentlemen normally operate? Because I will not go there, I cannot compete."

Forgan and Campbell united to assure him that they did not follow his profession, attractive and lucrative as it undoubtedly was. He took a great deal of convincing; as a matter of fact, he was never quite convinced. Politeness alone prompted him to drop the argument, saying only that it was a great pity that such singular natural gifts should be wasted. Apart from his profession he was shrewd, witty, and kindly; whenever the modelmakers went to Paris they made a point of seeing him and hearing his stories of the Parisian underworld and the very odd things which foreign visitors do when they are looking for amusement.

The two Englishmen reached Paris in the evening of June sixth and went at once to the Ambassador Hotel to claim their rooms. The evening was warm and sunny; Paris, recovering from the war, was enchanting. They took a quick glance round the dignified lounge of the Ambassador and a short drink at the bar. There was no one within sight who seriously resembled two Spaniards on a secret mission; they had five days to play with and the night was hardly begun. They went out, through the magic doors which open when they see you coming, into the Boulevard Haussmann and strolled along the dusty pavements in the violet evening light, listening delightedly to scraps of passing conversations above the incessant roar of the traffic—every motorist in Paris drives on his horn—staring into shopwindows, and engaging in complicated arithmetic to find out the prices of the goods. Lights appeared in windows, in the streets, and on the top of the Eiffel Tower; very slowly the night closed in. Forgan and Campbell, pleasantly exhilarated more with Paris than with wine, were sitting in a café halfway up the hill to the St. Sépulcre listening to Albert Baptiste.

"And after all that trouble," said Baptiste, finishing a story, "the man picked up the umbrella, bowed to each of the ladies separately, and went back to his hotel. I saw it, I myself."

"Well, he said he was only looking for his umbrella, didn't he?" said Forgan.

"Certainly he did, but the unbelievable thing is that it was true!"

A man and a woman passed their table on the way to the door. She smiled and nodded at Baptiste, who sprang to his feet, bowed from the waist, and said: "Bue' noches, señora."

"Are there many Spaniards in Paris?" asked Campbell idly.

"Not many, I think, they have not the money. That lady is a resident; she works at the Galeries Lafayette. They have assistants who between them can speak many languages, even Arabic, it is said. No, there are not many Spanish visitors, but that reminds me, there are a couple of Argentines, two men, whom I met the other night. There were four of them who came over, but they were in a little trouble and the police picked up two of them. I understand there was a little robbery in Buenos Aires and one of the victims was so annoying as to die; the rest are only in hospital. So the story goes, the Argentines did not confide in me personally. It appears that the police, when they arrested the other two, also seized upon most of the diamonds, so that my two poor acquaintances are hard pushed for money. I was asked if I knew anyone who wanted to buy two honest valid Argentine passports. I did not, at the moment, but there is usually a market for these things. The Argentines will never want them again, they hope; they will sell their nice new luggage, too, if they can in order to buy themselves complete outfits unmistakably French. So much less conspicuous, and you will understand that my poor acquaintances do not wish to be conspicuous. It is natural under the circumstances. You gentlemen have no interest in two valid Argentine passports and four suitcases made in Buenos Aires, complete as packed even to the toothbrushes?"

"So far as I can see at the moment," said Forgan, "Argentine passports have no place upon our menu; thank you very much for the courtesy which prompted the offer. Campbell and I spent over twenty years of our lives in the Argentine, we do not wish to be greedy. Let others occupy our space."

"I think you would only occupy two very small spaces if you went back to Buenos Aires on those passports," said Baptiste.

"In jail, you mean?" said Campbell. "I'm sure you're right. Besides, although we pride ourselves on being good mixers, Argentine society has had some rather queer additions since the war, hasn't it? Suppose we dropped into a bar for a refresher and came face to face with Hitler?"

"Unless it was a milk bar, you wouldn't," said Baptiste. "Are there milk bars in Buenos Aires?"

"We never saw one," said Forgan.

"But I cannot remember looking for one," said Campbell. "What do they do in milk bars?"

"I have no personal experience," said Baptiste, "but it is rumoured that they drink milk."

"Incredible," said Campbell, but Forgan said that he knew a man once who did that, and Baptiste asked what had happened to him.

"Horns sprouted upon his forehead and his wife left him," said Forgan gravely.

## 3 CAT–WITHOUT–TAIL

They breakfasted late the following morning, went out for a short stroll to air themselves, and came back to the Ambassador Hotel for a pre-lunch sherry. They were discussing, as they strolled through the lounge, what they would do that afternoon, and anyone near enough to be within earshot might have noticed that they were talking Spanish; it is natural to continue speaking in whatever language one has just been using, so they ordered their drinks in that language. Continental bartenders are accustomed to being addressed in every language of the more habitable parts of the globe, and this man had no difficulty in understanding and answering them. Presently they were aware, without looking round, that two men had stopped near them; the next minute a voice behind them offered apologies in Spanish. Forgan and Campbell turned in the friendliest manner possible and slipped off their high stools.

"The señores will find it difficult to forgive my unwarranted intrusion," said the stranger, "but it is very pleasant to hear one's own tongue in a foreign land."

"No apology is necessary," said Forgan genially. "We are gratified that the señor should have chosen to address us."

"My friend and I," said the first speaker, "can both speak

French sufficiently when we have to, you understand, but it is not a language in which we find ourselves at home. All the time we are aware that we are translating and there is the conscious effort to remember what we were told at school about the uses of the subjunctive."

"On holiday," said Campbell, "one does not wish to be trammelled with subjunctives."

"The real trouble, no doubt," said the second Spaniard gloomily, "is that it is too long since we were at school."

"You would not wish to return, señor?" said Forgan. "No, nor I. But the thought appears to depress you; dare I offer sherry to Spaniards? Or perhaps there is something else you would prefer." He caught the bartender's eye and a discussion upon vintages followed.

The Spaniard who had spoken first was a tall slim man whose black hair had retreated some distance from his forehead and turned silver at the temples. He had good features, a distinguished appearance, and the unembarrassed manners of an assured social position. The other was a small stout man with a bulbous nose and a permanently worried expression. They were not men one would have expected to be travelling together.

The sherry question having been settled, the tall Spaniard reverted to the topic of language. "I think—am I right?— you two gentlemen are not from Spain itself, but from the Argentine, is it not so?"

"Our unfortunate accent," murmured Forgan, and the other hastened to apologize.

"Not at all, not at all. One does but notice those minor differences which I find so interesting."

"Has the señor visited Buenos Aires?" asked Campbell.

"Not yet, but it is my ambition to go there someday. Perhaps next year. A beautiful city, is it not?"

"Beautiful," said Forgan with emotion, "beautiful. The houses are palaces, the gardens are like those in Paradise, the streets are gay, and life is a song. The women walk like empresses and have hearts like loving children——"

"Golden hearts," said Campbell dreamily, "pure gold is what they have at heart."

"The señores are poets," said the tall Spaniard.

"No, no, we have no words," said Forgan humbly. "We are but bond slaves of beauty, lackeys of loveliness."

"Groomsmen of grace," murmured Campbell, gazing absently into the distance. He lifted his glass as for a toast, kissed the rim, and swallowed the contents.

After which it was with a sense of anticlimax that the tall Spaniard introduced the subject of what they ought to see in Paris. "I have been here but once before in my life, I blush to say it. I was a boy of fourteen; my tutor brought me. We stayed with a most correct family and, to be frank with you, I remember nothing but the circus. And you, Piccione?"

"Never before," said the small Spaniard, "never."

"How long do the señores propose to stay?" asked Forgan.

"Alas, only five days. We must leave again on Sunday the eleventh."

Forgan, Campbell, and the bartender went into committee forthwith and laid out for them a series of tours and visits of inspection. The Louvre, Notre Dame, the tomb of Napoleon, the Ste. Chapelle, the Morgue, the Catacombs. Versailles, the Petit Trianon, Les Halles at five in the morning, the Café de l'Enfer at midnight.

The Spaniards brightened up a little at this last suggestion, and Forgan added quickly that they need have no qualms, the place was nowadays of the utmost respectability and the most unsophisticated visitor would be quite safe there. "It is but the décor which is designed to amaze," he said.

The bartender came to the rescue with a suggestion that the Spaniards should start by making a couple of motorcoach tours about the city. He produced a leaflet on the subject. There was one tour of the new part and another of the old part. "By this means the señores will, in a very short time, obtain a general idea of Paris which would otherwise take weeks to acquire. The señores can then decide what most interests them and arrange their visits accordingly. There is a tour this afternoon at half-past fourteen hours and the reception clerk would book seats for them."

The Spaniards seized upon this suggestion, disengaged themselves gracefully, and hurried off towards the reception desk. Forgan and Campbell finished their sherry and walked leisurely across the lounge to the dining room.

"Since one is Piccione," began Forgan in a low tone.

"The other is D'Almeida," finished Campbell. "And they are going away on the eleventh."

"They're the blokes," said Forgan. "If we give them the rest of today and most of tomorrow to absorb culture, I should think they'd be ready to be amused by tomorrow night."

"D'Almeida is the sort of man who might really like pictures."

"Yes, but Piccione isn't. Tomorrow evening will see him through."

Late the following afternoon D'Almeida and Piccione were found sitting in two of the most comfortable chairs in the lounge, not so much sitting as sunk into them. Their eyes were slightly glazed but not with drink; Campbell, waiting in the lounge for Forgan, went over and spoke to them.

"I hope you have had an amusing time," he said.

"Interesting," said D'Almeida, "very interesting."

"Instructive," groaned Piccione, "very instructive."

"Why," said Campbell with a smile, "wasn't that what you wanted?"

Piccione closed his eyes and at that moment Forgan came up to them.

"I hope you have had a pleasant time," he said.

"Hush," said Campbell, "our friends are tired."

"This sight-seeing," said Forgan sympathetically. "It tries the feet severely."

Piccione waggled his disconsolately, but D'Almeida gathered his forces together and sat upright.

"But the señores are standing," he said in a horrified voice. "Chairs—let me——"

"I beg," said Forgan, and brought chairs for himself and Campbell.

"I think that what my friend and I are suffering from," said D'Almeida, "is not so much physical fatigue as mental exhaustion. One owes it to the treasures we have seen yesterday and today to spread wide the eager arms of appreciation——"

"But the mere posture is exhausting," said Campbell. "Even the patriarch Moses, a tough guy if ever there was one, found it so."

"What the señores need," said Forgan, "is a little innocent relaxation."

"You anticipate my very words," said D'Almeida. "We should like to see something of the justly famous night life of Paris, to go to a cabaret show perhaps, to drop into a café here, a *bistro* there, the *brasserie* on the corner. Not the places to which they conduct the tourists but the small places to which Parisians themselves resort."

"Well, why don't you?" said Forgan. "There is no difficulty. Just turn your faces towards Montmartre and keep on."

Piccione opened his eyes and displayed interest.

"But there is a difficulty, señor," said D'Almeida.

"Difficulties exist in order to be overcome, señor," said Campbell.

"If it is not a private matter——" began Forgan.

"Put briefly," said D'Almeida, "it is this. We are men sent upon a mission of some importance and we represent in our unworthy persons the dignity of those who sent us. Suppose there were a little trouble, a minor fracas, and the police came, demanding to see papers; suppose we were summoned in our own names as witnesses——"

"It would not do," said Forgan. "The señores are gentlemen of the most delicate sense of honour and they are perfectly right. It would not do at all."

"In Madrid," pursued D'Almeida, "if it were desirable to furnish a gentleman with different papers for occasions when he rightly wishes to remain anonymous—in Madrid, I say, we should know where to go. But here, in Paris, we are strangers, we are as children."

There was a short pause.

"It should be possible," said Forgan slowly. "Yes. Listen, señores. My friend and I have an appointment in ten minutes' time; it will not take long, but we must keep it. Let the señores rest a little longer and then dine; when we return we will see what can be done."

Campbell and Forgan left the hotel with the rapid strides of men who are pressed for time; when they were well away Campbell said: "Those Argentine passports, I suppose?"

"If they're not sold. And their luggage too; I've had a whale of an idea."

Forgan and Campbell returned to the Ambassador two hours later and asked if D'Almeida and Piccione were in the hotel. The desk clerk said that they were in their rooms and had left word that the gentlemen were to be taken up to them at once. The desk clerk bowed, the lift boy sprang to attention, and the lift whirled up to the third floor.

The Spaniards certainly intended to be comfortable. They had a small suite of two excellent bedrooms with a bathroom between, all shut off from the passage by an outer door. Campbell knocked upon it, Piccione opened the door, and D'Almeida called to them to come in and be welcome.

Forgan said that he and his friend had been trying to get some passports for the señores but had unfortunately been unsuccessful. "It seems that Spanish or Argentine passports are hard to come by," he said. "We were offered Czech, Greek, and Iranian, but we did not think that they would suit. We therefore——"

"My dear friends," said D'Almeida, "the trouble we have given you——"

"Not at all, a pleasure. We therefore thought that the obvious plan was to lend you ours for the evening. We are

44

not going out tonight—we are expecting friends—if you return them to us in the morning that will do well." Forgan unfolded two sheets of stiff paper, grubby from much handling, worn through at the folds, and stained with various vintages. The worst stains had been hastily dried before an electric fire in Baptiste's room, and it was upon his carpet that the photographs had been rubbed until they were nearly unrecognizable. "I apologize for their condition," said Forgan; "there was a farewell party on the ship. This is my friend's," he added, handing over a passport in the lovely name of Giacomo Xavier Bonamour, "and this is mine, Diego Cierra, at your service. Both of Buenos Aires, as you see."

"I hardly like——" began D'Almeida, hesitating.

"To touch them," finished Campbell. "It is no wonder, they are a matter for tongs."

"Indeed, no, Señor Bonamour," said D'Almeida warmly. "I was only thinking what an appalling disaster it would be if we lost them—suppose our pockets were picked——"

"It is simple," said Forgan cheerfully. "It is but to go to the Argentine Legation, fortified by your company as witness to our respectability, and get new ones. They will at least be clean."

"We will tell the Legation a sad story about how we came to lose them," said Campbell. "We will each of us devise a story and tell whichever one is the most worthy of belief. Besides, why should you lose them? Put them in an inside pocket."

"I cannot see why we should lose them," said Piccione.

"Very well," said D'Almeida, "I give in. We will borrow your passports, señores, and if any mischance should come of our having done so I, Alfonso Demetrio d'Almeida, will deal with it. Will our own be safe in these drawers, do you think?"

"I should hide them," said Forgan. "The hotel staff come in when they will."

Piccione took both the Spanish passports and looked round the room for somewhere to hide them.

"Under the mattress?"

"They turn down the beds," said Campbell. "Heaven knows what that process involves, but something happens to the beds."

"In the loop of the curtain?"

"They draw the curtains," said D'Almeida. "I noticed that last night."

"I remember now," said Forgan with an obvious effort of memory, "a hiding place of which I was once told. Now, you have a private bathroom and in it is also a lavatory cistern, no doubt. Yes, well, you lift off the lid of the cistern (they are never fastened down) and put your passports inside the lid, fastening them there with cellophane tape. No one looks for papers in a cistern of water. I have a roll of tape, if——"

"I have some," said D'Almeida, hunting in a small attaché case. "Piccione, the cistern lid. Señores, your inexhaustible ingenuity staggers me."

The passports were put together; at the last moment the Spaniards added their travellers' cheques to the packet and gleefully stowed it away. Forgan and Campbell stood back and looked on with the indulgent air of uncles watching the children enjoy themselves.

"To add a final item to our list of indebtedness to you,"

said D'Almeida, "have you any suggestions to make as to where we should go?"

"Anywhere in the Montmartre district should prove amusing," said Campbell. "You know where that is? Turn left when you leave the hotel, take the third turning to the left, and carry straight on. As for any special places . . ." He paused and looked at Forgan, who named a café running a cabaret show and a *bistro* where the brandy was a matter for poetry.

"Talking about poets," said Campbell, and told them where to find some.

"Or if you like pictures," said Forgan, "modern French art, some of them will be valuable someday," and he described where to find them.

"But the absolute place——" began Campbell at the same moment as Forgan started: "The one spot you mustn't miss——" And they looked at each other and laughed.

"Continue, señores, I beg," said D'Almeida. "This place?"

"Le Chat sans Queue," said Forgan. "It is a bit warm, but we are men of the world and our wives are not with us."

"The what?" asked Piccione.

"El Gato sin Rabo," said Campbell, translating. "The Tailless Cat. Whatever else you don't see, you must go there. If only our friends weren't coming," he added to Forgan, who sighed.

"Never mind, we can go there tomorrow night," he said. "It is not necessary to arrive there too early, señores; the later, the more cheerful. I will tell you exactly where it is," and he did so in some detail while Piccione made notes.

They saw the Spaniards off at the door of the hotel and

stood there for a few minutes after they were out of sight.

"Well, I hope they remember all that," said Forgan. "Now, if Baptiste does his stuff properly——"

Some hours later, well after midnight, Forgan and Campbell strolled up a narrow twisting street in the Montmartre district towards a café which displayed in the middle of its window a coloured transparency of a bright pink cat with large blue spots and no vestige of a tail. They did not enter; as they passed they caught the eye of a short stout gentleman sitting at a table just inside the door. He appeared to be watching for them and came out at once to join them.

"All goes well, messieurs. The Spanish gentlemen are asleep. Look! In the far corner."

They peered in at the doorway. D'Almeida was sprawled forwards across a table and one long arm hung down till its fingers touched the floor; Piccione, who had been sitting on a padded seat against the wall, was lying along it with his knees up. Nobody in the café, which was fairly full, was taking the slightest notice of them.

"Well done," said Forgan softly. "Baptiste! You left them the passports?"

"But certainly they have the passports. As for the rest, I thank you."

Campbell said it was nothing, and Baptiste courteously contradicted him. "I will not say it was a fortune, but it was far from nothing," he said. "Here is the key to their rooms in the hotel."

The Englishman took the key, nodded, and walked away. The street led into a small square where there was a policeman standing about looking ornamental. They went up to him and asked in English what the procedure was if one wished to report the theft of a wallet containing money. The policeman understood English if the words used were simple and slowly spoken, so Campbell tried again.

"Men take my money," he said. "In wallet, like that." Forgan showed his. "I want to tell some man official."

The policeman got that. "You know who stole, no?"

Campbell nodded. "Think so, yes. Two men"—he held up two fingers—"two Argentines."

"Two Argentines," repeated the policeman.

"At least they said they were Argentines, but they may have been stringing us along," said Forgan, and the policeman turned a blank stare upon him.

"You too fast enough," said Campbell reprovingly. "This gentleman no get."

"Sorry, I'm sure," said Forgan.

"Come," said Campbell to the policeman. "Men in this café."

"Eh?" said the policeman. "You know where men is, yes?"

"Yes. When they go, we find money gone. We follow. Long way. Many places. Now there," and Campbell pointed to Le Chat sans Queue.

"*Un moment,*" said the policeman, and signalled to a colleague, who came quickly. They had a short conference in rapid French of which Forgan caught only the phrase "*ces Anglais imbéciles,*" and the first policeman turned to Campbell again.

"Come," he said. "Show."

They moved off together to the doorway of Le Chat sans Queue, and Campbell took the policeman by the arm.

"In there," he said. "At back. Far back. Why," he added

in a tone of surprise, "they're asleep! Or ill. Gone bye-byes, yes?"

The policeman disengaged himself from Campbell and said: "Wait. Wait. Compris?"

"Compree," said Campbell, nodding eagerly. The two policemen marched into the café and along the centre gangway towards the table at the back. Baptiste was no longer there, but several of the other customers, seeing the police uniforms, suddenly remembered important engagements and went out quickly; Forgan and Campbell were lost to view behind them.

## 4  SURPRISE IN THE CISTERN

Some time in the small hours it was reported at police headquarters that the other two Argentines who had escaped arrest when the first two were captured a week earlier had been found in a café in Montmartre. That is, their identity was not yet proved beyond doubt, but they carried the passports of the missing men and such words as they were able to utter were in the Spanish language. They had been doped. Remedial measures restored an uncertain degree of consciousness to the prisoners, who denied indignantly that they were the missing Argentines. When asked why, if that were the case, they were carrying those passports, they held their aching heads and became evasive. Pressed further, they gave the names of D'Almeida and Piccione and said that they were staying at the Hotel Ambassador, suite number so-and-so. They were left in peace for a time while enquiries were made at the hotel.

The police sergeant making the enquiry asked to see their rooms and was taken to them. He found two suitcases in each room; they were only partially unpacked and their clothes were lying untidily about or had been hastily thrown into drawers. (This was a libel upon D'Almeida, who was naturally tidy, but Forgan and Campbell had had

a busy night with so much to do and little time to do it.)
The policeman particularly noticed the small labels inside
the lids of the suitcases which stated the names and ad-
dresses of various shops in Buenos Aires, Argentina. One
of those in D'Almeida's room announced also that it was
made of "best Argentine leather." The suits also, heavily
padded on the shoulders, bore the labels of Buenos Aires
firms.

He looked further and found in the bottom of a suitcase
in Piccione's room a thing which Forgan in his haste had
overlooked. It was a small tortoise-shell-and-gold cigarette
case with an inscription on the inside, "Juanita from
Annibale," and a date. It was on the list of stolen articles;
the list had been circulated, and the Argentines, who had
brought it away with the rest of the proceeds of the robbery, had found it unsalable at the moment; it was too rec-
ognizable. In the hurry of selling their luggage they had
forgotten that it was there, but the police sergeant recognized it at once from the description. He left the rooms
as they were, locked them up and also sealed them, and departed for headquarters, whistling under his breath a charming little ditty which begins "Dites-moi, grand'mère," to
which he always resorted when he was pleased.

Confronted with this testimony, the prisoners became
even more emphatic in their denials and said that they
were Spaniards from Madrid, not Argentines from Buenos
Aires, and that their own passports were in their rooms at
the hotel. Asked why, if that were the case, the sergeant
of police had not found them when he searched the rooms,
the prisoners said that the passports had been hidden to
prevent their falling into the hands of unauthorized per-

sons. The police superintendent, who was conducting the enquiry, a man never at his best before breakfast, took this remark as a reflection on the police, and D'Almeida had considerable difficulty in soothing him. Eventually the prisoners undertook, if they were allowed to return to the hotel, to produce their own passports.

When they arrived there under escort they both said with all the emphasis they could command—they were still feeling anything but well—that the luggage was not theirs although it was labelled with their names in their own handwriting. (Campbell, thorough in all things, had soaked their labels off their own luggage and stuck it upon the Argentine cases.) While D'Almeida was arguing this point Piccione asked to be allowed to go to the bathroom. The detective who had him in charge agreed, but put his foot in the bathroom door to prevent its being locked.

A moment later he heard an odd scraping noise which reminded him of flowerpots being stacked, for his father was a market gardener. He opened the door to see Piccione in the act of lifting down the lid of the cistern.

"What are you doing there?"

Piccione turned the lid over, looked inside it, and then set the lid down on the floor and burst into tears.

"*Los pasaportes,*" he sobbed, his French deserting him, "the passports, they were here and they are not."

D'Almeida and the other detective came in.

"What is all this?"

D'Almeida explained how and where the passports had been hidden. The detectives looked at each other and then one of them climbed up and looked into the cistern. What he saw appeared to surprise him, for he uttered a grunt, pulled up his right sleeve, and plunged his arm into the water.

"Are they there, then?" asked D'Almeida anxiously.

The detective drew out from the cistern two small boxes, one covered with leather and the other with velvet, such as ladies use to carry their trinkets when they are travelling. When opened they were seen to contain jewellery; nothing very startling in value, but good of their kind and eminently salable.

"These," said the senior detective, "answer the description of goods stolen in a small robbery within this hotel last night. If so, they can readily be identified."

(Forgan had watched two ladies go down to dinner the evening before, had abstracted the housemaid's passkey for a few moments, and just snatched the first thing that offered.)

D'Almeida put his hands over his face and staggered back against the wall; Piccione's legs gave way and he sank down upon the floor. In the face of this circumstantial evidence it was in vain that they told their story about being lent passports for the evening by two friendly Argentines named Cierra and Bonamour who were also staying at the Ambassador. The detectives laughed shortly and removed the prisoners.

"But," said Piccione plaintively, "why does all this have to happen to *us*?"

It had been arranged that Forgan and Campbell should stay at the Dom Hotel in Cologne. They went, therefore, at their leisure, arriving very late one night and taking up the accommodation reserved for D'Almeida and Piccione.

They had passed the frontier on their own passports, since frontier officials are people who really examine passports and compare photographs with the faces they purport to reproduce; also, there was some rapid juggling with labels on luggage between the frontier and Cologne. Reception clerks in hotels merely take a passport in order to copy accurately the traveller's name and home address into their records; establishment of identity is no business of theirs and their own work keeps them quite busy enough.

On the morning after their arrival Forgan and Campbell slept late, breakfasted at leisure, and strolled out into the Dom Square shortly before midday; Spaniards are not as a rule early risers. The first thing they saw when they came out through the revolving doors was the familiar figure of Tommy Hambledon sitting at a table by the door of a small public house near by, drinking beer and talking to two friends.

Forgan and Campbell stood on the pavement and stared about them; it was the first time they had ever been in Germany, and Cologne Cathedral, always an amazing sight, is still more so now that it towers above ruins. They remained by the door, talking and pointing out things to each other, until they saw Hambledon rise to his feet, feeling in his trouser pocket for money. They then walked slowly away towards the open-air café in the square, where they sat down at a table and waited for Hambledon to join them.

"What the devil d'you mean," he said, " 'we are the Spaniards'? Where are they?"

"They are on their way to Buenos Aires," said Forgan, "on a slow cargo boat, *La Luz de la Luna*. They are quite safe and well; they are in charge of the captain."

"We saw that in the Paris papers," added Campbell. "That they had sailed in her, I mean."

Hambledon looked from one to the other. "What is all this? Some of your devilments, I know."

"Oh, that is unkind," said Forgan reproachfully. "They said it was their life's ambition to see Buenos Aires before they died, so they went."

"We may have helped them a little," said Campbell. "Do you think we did, Forgan?"

"I like to think so," said Forgan dreamily. "This helping hand to the passing stranger, what does it cost us? Nothing. And yet——"

"Come on," said Tommy. "Out with it."

"It all started," said Forgan, "because we thought we would enjoy a few days in Paris on our way here, so we drew our holiday money and went."

They told Hambledon the whole tale and he leaned back in his chair and laughed till he cried.

"You told us," finished Forgan, "that the Spaniards were not personally known to their contacts here, so we thought we would do instead. They had some very helpful notes in their luggage; we think we can talk intelligently to whoever meets us."

"And if we get out of our depth," said Campbell, "we can just be dark and mysterious, can't we?"

"You may end by getting your throats cut," said Hambledon.

"That, in itself, would be a new experience," said Forgan.

"It would be one I should not care to repeat," admitted Campbell. "And yourself? I hope that you are having a pleasant holiday and getting some interesting photographs?" There was a waiter hovering near by for a repetition of their order.

"Not very interesting so far," said Hambledon. "I hope to get some later, perhaps, when I've had a little more time here."

"You want to look round first, of course," said Forgan. "Do you know this place at all?"

"I used to know it very well; in fact, I lived here at one time many years ago. I don't recognize much of it now."

"It looks as though there had been drastic alterations," said Campbell. "If you do get any good photographs we shall be interested to see them. Will you have another glass of wine? The waiter seems to think we ought. I don't know what it was, but it was very nice." He called up the waiter and renewed the order in his extraordinary German, and the man went away to fetch it. "While we have a moment's privacy, what comes next?"

"Sit tight and wait till you are approached," said Hambledon. "I am making a few contacts which may be useful, but the first move is with the other side. If you want to get in touch with me, ring up the Gürzenich Hotel. But I shall be about and we shall meet. Be careful, I expect they've got somebody planted in your hotel and probably in mine too. I don't know."

The waiter came back with the wine to find them discussing cameras. "If you want to buy one," Hambledon was saying, "there's the Photohaus Stein in the Hohestrasse, down there——"

Hambledon went back to his hotel through the ruined area and along the Unter Goldschmied. This part of the town, between the Hohestrasse and the river, had had

nothing whatever done to it since the raids except a per-
functory clearing of some of the roads by the simple process of throwng the rubble to either side or shovelling it into
bomb holes. It was quite desolate and uninhabited, the
gaunt ruin of the Rathaus towered over it, and but few
people were ever seen there; indeed, there was nothing for
which anyone would wish to go there unless he wished
to pray among the ruins, and the Cologne people did not
seem to do that. Yet that district had an odd attraction for
Hambledon; his feet seemed to carry him there of their
own accord.

A little way along the Unter Goldschmied one comes to
the Laurenzplatz, an open space where there was once a
statue of which only the plinth is now standing. There
were two girls at the corner here, apparently peering across
the Platz with their backs to Hambledon. He remembered
Spelmann's reference to "girls who frolic among the ruins"
and his face hardened; at that moment they turned and
came towards him in haste. Before they reached him they
turned off up a little path which ran between the rubble
heaps, broke into a run, and were immediately out of sight.

A man came, walking slowly, across the Laurenzplatz;
it seemed that the girls were anxious to avoid him, which
struck Hambledon as a little odd. The man was very obviously English and about thirty years of age; he walked as
though he had no particular destination in view and even
at a distance he had an air of depression and discourage-
ment. He passed Hambledon quite close, appearing scarcely
to notice him, so absorbed he was in his own unhappy
thoughts.

Hambledon had lunch at his hotel and was standing in

the hall, lighting a cigarette and wondering what he could most usefully do until the other side made some move, when a man addressed him with some comment about the weather which Hambledon answered mechanically.

"The Herr finds matters of interest for his camera in our poor Köln?"

"Oh yes," said Tommy. "There are views of the Cathedral which must have been quite unobtainable before all this happened."

"That is so. No doubt that is so. But the Herr will forgive a word of kindly warning?"

Hambledon looked at him and the man went on:

"The Herr has been seen several times to walk along the Unter Goldschmied among the ruins."

"Well? What of it?"

"It is not very wise. Why go there? No one could find it pleasant. It is much pleasanter where the shops and the people are, is it not, or along the quays beside the Rhine?"

"What are you warning me against?" said Hambledon bluntly; in his character of English tourist he felt that it was natural to be blunt.

"It is dangerous to wander among the ruins. That is all. There are most attractive coach tours, let the Herr entertain himself in that way. The desk clerk has all the particulars."

"It's an idea, certainly," said Hambledon amiably, and strolled off to consult the desk clerk about tours, of which there appeared to be quite a choice both by road and river. Hambledon looked at leaflets until the man who had addressed him walked out of the door, and then asked the clerk who he was.

"The gentleman who spoke to you? I don't know. He is not a resident and I don't remember seeing him before. Many people come here for meals, or to call on our guests; we don't know them all, naturally."

Tommy nodded. "Seems a pleasant fellow. He suggested these tours. I think I'll go one of these days."

## 5   *UNTER GOLDSCHMIED*

The next morning Hambledon strolled into the Dom Square and encountered Spelmann, the private detective, walking in haste. He wore a hat, which was unusual for him, a black hat and a rather better suit with a crease down the trousers. He saw Hambledon and rushed up to him.

"I have not a moment, I am on my way to the official enquiry. I only wanted to tell you that there was a post-mortem on poor Karl and there was no trace of any narcotic."

"Indeed. Then I was wrong, that's all. I often am," said Tommy cheerfully.

"I also," said Spelmann, turning to go. "See you again soon, over there, eh?" He jerked his thumb towards the Muserkeller and went hurriedly away.

The next person to greet Hambledon was the photographer, anxious for his approval of the photographs delivered that morning at the Gürzenich Hotel. "Not so good as I could have wished. The Herr appears to have moved slightly. The features seem a little blurred, though the rest of it is sharp enough. If I might be permitted to try again——"

"No, no," said Hambledon, "there is no need. Indeed, my features are of the type which is all the better for a little blurring, in my opinion. I like the photographs." He had, of course, moved intentionally; it was impossible not to be photographed if one wanted to make a friend of the photographer, but that was no reason for allowing one's face to be too recognizably recorded. They stood there talking. There was no sign of Forgan and Campbell this morning, but a few minutes later the Englishman whom Hambledon had seen in the Laurenzplatz walked slowly along in front of the Excelsior Hotel, which faced the Dom Hotel across the square. He passed along under the gay red-and-white-striped awning as though he did not care where he went, and turned left; Hambledon, prompted by his incurably enquiring mind, wandered after him.

The streets just east of the Cathedral are by no means so completely ruined as those on the other sides; it was refreshing to find buildings still in occupation and shops as they were before. The Englishman turned into a café and sat down at a table; the place was fairly full and it was natural for Hambledon, following him in, to sit at the same table. Tommy took his camera out of its case and played with the aperture adjustment and the focussing; he was very plainly unused to it and he hoped that, if the other man were a photographer, he would not be able to resist offering advice. However, he took very little notice.

The waiter came for the order and the Englishman asked for coffee; when it came to Tommy's turn he spoke very broken German and made heavy weather of explaining that he wanted his coffee with whipped cream on the top, not ordinary smooth cream served separately. The waiter did not understand. Tommy said, "Oh dear," in English and tried again with no better result.

This time the Englishman did rise to the bait. He told the waiter what was wanted. Hambledon was very grateful indeed and said that it was evident that his rescuer was either brilliant at languages or had spent much time in Germany.

"I learnt German at school," he answered, "and put in a lot of practice here with the Army. I was on Traffic Control here for quite a long time."

"You don't live here now, then?"

"Oh no, I live in London. No, I just ran over for a few days to look up some people I used to know here."

"I think the people here must have had a terrible time," said Tommy sympathetically, "though they seem to be pulling themselves together wonderfully. The things in the shops simply amaze me. Of course, I know nothing about their private lives."

"Some of them are rather unsettled; there is a good deal of private unhappiness." The Englishman fidgeted with the cruet on the table, changing the little pots over to see if they fitted in each other's holes. "I hardly know how to put it, things have changed in a way I didn't expect and not always for the better. I—I don't know——" He looked eagerly at Hambledon, upon whom it suddenly dawned that the man was aching to talk to somebody.

"I'm sorry to hear that," said Tommy. "I hope that you found your own friends well and happy."

"That's it. I found them well as far as that goes, but—there's something wrong. You see, when I got back here —— Why should I bore you with this? Let's talk about something else."

"No. Let's talk about this. I am not easily bored, believe

me, and sometimes to tell the story helps to clear one's own mind."

"Well, you've asked for it, and I tell you, if I can't talk to somebody soon it will drive me mad. When I was billeted here on Traffic Control I met a girl." His voice dropped on the last word, and Tommy said to himself that this was the thimble which had the pea under it. "She and I—she was a very nice girl, I liked her quite a lot. I saw a good deal of her, being billeted at the house and all that. When I was moved on I used to write and she answered, and so on. Sure this isn't boring you?"

"Not at all, please go on."

"When I was demobilized I had to find a job and then work it up a bit, and so on. I went on writing to her; one couldn't get out here in person—— To cut a long story short, she left off writing about a year ago, so I came out to see why. Her father and mother are dead and the house was sold or something; anyway, there are strangers living there. They couldn't tell me anything about Magda, where she lived, or anything. Then I saw her."

He stopped for so long that Hambledon thought it only kind to help him on.

"Did you speak to her?"

"I didn't get a chance; she ran away and I lost her in the ruins."

Another long pause, till suddenly he looked up with a face so twisted with grief that Hambledon averted his eyes.

"She—I don't like it—if she's doing what it looks as—— I don't know what to do. I did stop her one day and she held me off. Told me for God's sake to go away. Said she couldn't—I can't believe it. I won't."

After a moment's silence Hambledon said: "You'll have to make sure one way or the other or you'll never have peace of mind again."

"I know. That's not all. This morning I got this note." He took a letter from his pocket and passed it across the table. Hambledon thought that his German, though bad, might be equal to reading a short note and picked it up. It was written on a slip of plain white paper.

> Herr George Yeoman. Keep away from the Unter Goldschmied or you will be sorry. This is a warning. Go away from Köln and never come back. Danger for you in the Unter Goldschmied.

"Is this her writing?" asked Tommy.

"No. Never saw it before."

"Are you going away?"

"Am I hell! I've got a room in a flat here and I'm staying till I clear this up."

Hambledon nodded. "Look here, Mr. Yeoman—that is your name? Yes, well, mine's Hambledon. I'm staying at the Gürzenich Hotel, you probably know it. I'll see you again. Let me know if anything happens and particularly if I can do anything to help you."

"Thank you very much indeed," said Yeoman sincerely. "It's bucked me up no end, meeting you. I'll let you know what happens."

Hambledon administered encouragement, left Yeoman looking almost cheerful, and walked thoughtfully away. Two warnings to keep clear of the Unter Goldschmied; there was certainly something odd about that district. He wondered how many more people had been warned off that course. Englishmen are notorious for poking their noses into whatever arouses their curiosity; the people of Cologne, if they had any idea that there was something afoot, would no doubt make a point of avoiding the place, and very wise, too. Poor Yeoman's Magda was, no doubt, one of the two girls who were hiding from him yesterday; Hambledon had seen them plainly at short range and remembered them both distinctly. One was short and fair and rather plump; the other was tall and slim, dark-haired with a pale complexion, well-marked eyebrows, good features, and a certain amount of natural dignity. Hambledon, who was old-fashioned in some respects, mentally described her as "more of a lady" than the other.

He returned to the Dom Square in time to see the backs of Forgan and Campbell as they turned down by the side of their hotel in the direction of the river. He went down a parallel street, came out by the river just in front of his friends, and walked away from them. The riverbank here is a series of quays for the busy river traffic of Cologne, but it is also a promenade with trees, seats, and here and there a small café. The travelling Englishman always wonders how on earth the numerous cafés in Continental towns ever manage to make a living; in Cologne there are even more than usual. Here, owing to the destruction of house property, most people who work in Cologne live outside it and come in for the day; they eat and rest in cafés and so do the inhabitants of the city itself, where overcrowded houses make privacy impossible and even cooking a difficulty. Hence the innumerable cafés, restaurants, beer shops, sausage stalls, lemonade and coffee sellers whom one sees at intervals of a few yards wherever a shelter can be found or improvised to keep off the rain, and they all make a living.

Hambledon turned into a pleasant place which had probably been there before the war, found a table behind a row of pot plants, ordered coffee, and sat down. Presently Forgan and Campbell came in, also ordered coffee, and sat at the table next his. They were talking Spanish to each other, and one of them wanted to know what were the buildings on the opposite bank, at Köln-Deutz. They appealed to Hambledon, who leaned forward and replied politely that they used to be exhibition buildings of some kind but what they were used for now he could not say. The ice between strangers having been broken, Hambledon transferred his coffee cup to their table and suggested objects of interest such as would attract the intelligent tourist. The waiter moved away, and Tommy asked if anything had happened yet.

"Not exactly happened," said Forgan cautiously. "Something has rather significantly failed to happen."

"Thanks to our powers of observation and intelligent foresight," said Campbell. "After you left us at midday yesterday we had lunch at the hotel and then went up to unpack our things in comfort and at leisure."

"We had time," said Forgan, "to admire the design of our suitcases. We all know how tiresome it is to have breakables broken by baggage-hurling porters. Our suitcases have been specially designed to prevent that. The sides and the bottoms are quite thickly padded. A felt want, as they say."

"The idea should be more generally adopted," said Campbell. "That treasured bottle of cognac, that little flask of eau de cologne for the wife, if any——"

"The pottery from Quimper," said Forgan, "that precious cup of Imperial Meissen, what are they? Fragments, as a rule."

"We had an argument as to what the padding consisted of," said Campbell, "so we cut a tiny slit where it wouldn't show and had a look."

"Such a surprise," said Forgan innocently. "Wads and wads of German hundred-mark notes. Some curious mistake somewhere, no doubt. The factory which made this luggage——"

"What did you do with the money?" asked Tommy.

"Packed it all up in a neat parcel and had it parked in the hotel safe," said Forgan. "It is so immoral to leave money about as a temptation to underpaid hotel servants and others."

"Particularly the others," said Campbell. "We obtained a tube of adhesive and stuck the lining neatly back in place. We arranged some clothes in the cases in a manner seemingly haphazard but actually memorized and went out for a walk to see a Roman gateway in a street whose name I have forgotten. It stood up to bombing much better than many more modern erections; we were enthralled. Then we had dinner in a restaurant and wandered slowly home to find that some conscienceless brigand had not only upset the things in our suitcases but torn the linings far worse than we did."

"So we had to sit up half the night mending them again," said Forgan. "I am not a fussy man, but I cannot abide untidy luggage."

"You know," said Campbell, "supposing for the sake of argument that we had brought that money as a gift

68

to some—er—charitable organization and they had deliberately stolen it before we had a chance to present it, we should be justly irritated, don't you agree?"

"I do indeed," said Tommy. "In fact, when anybody does approach you about your pet charity, you might quite well be justly irritated, as you say. Take a high hand and ask them what the hell they mean by it. I should. There's nothing like putting people where you want 'em."

"I suppose they are the same people," said Forgan thoughtfully. "The burglars and the official receivers so to speak?"

"I don't think that matters," said Hambledon. "If not, it'll give our friends something to worry about, and that's always a good idea."

"Had we thought of it," said Campbell, "we might have taught the intruder a lesson with a simple device of, for example, spring mousetraps. Are there any joke shops in Cologne? One of those batlike things you wind up and put in a book; when released it flutters madly in your face."

"Or something which utters a loud yell when disturbed," said Forgan.

"Or merely howls for the police," said Tommy. "I'm afraid it's too late; they're not likely to come again. And the drawback of that sort of thing is that you're liable to forget it and catch yourself. I did that once when I connected a door handle to the electricity supply."

"Tiresome," said Forgan. "By the way, we've got a lot of what looks like quite genuine data about supplying oranges from Valencia. Do you suppose we're expected to call on real green grocers on real business? Or is that only the method of approach?"

"We haven't got any samples," said Campbell.

"Let it ride," said Hambledon. "I don't believe the fruit business is genuine; there's plenty of fruit in Cologne, and imported at that."

"I've seen it," said Forgan. "Barrows laden with bananas have these eyes beheld. I thought I had delusions."

"What about you?" said Campbell. "Or is it tactless to ask whether you've come upon anything yet?"

"Frankly, I don't think I have," said Hambledon. "There is a little funny business going on, but the chances are that it's nothing to do with us. It may be black-marketeering or drugs or some such racket; more probably, I think."

"It is a long time since breakfast," said Forgan, getting to his feet as the waiter came forward. "The Herr's great courtesy in so fully explaining things to a pair of ignorant travellers will materially contribute to the pleasure of our visit."

"We cannot thank him enough," said Campbell.

"The pleasure was entirely mine," said Hambledon.

He started back to his hotel through the ruined area but avoiding the road called the Unter Goldschmied, taking photographs here and there mainly of the ragged shell of the Town Hall's fifteenth-century tower from various points of view. He saw nothing of the girls—perhaps it was too early in the day for them—but he did have a few words with an employe of the Cologne electricity supply company making a tour of the street lamps.

"You'd hardly believe it," said the man, "but the electric mains were scarcely damaged. Too far underground, no doubt. So, wherever there isn't a pile of rubble yards high over where the street lamps used to be, we just puts up a pole and a lamp and connects up again. You'll have seen several about here and there. Funny, isn't it?"

"It is strange," said Hambledon. "Do you mean to tell me that under all these acres of rubble there are the faithful electric cables still running, probably with meters still on the ends of 'em?"

The man nodded. "Of course the house wiring is all bust to blazes, but when people put up little shops and that like you see along the Hohestrasse, there's no trouble about light and that." He posed, grinning, for a photograph before one of his pole lamp-standards and went on his way.

"Supposing," said Hambledon to a young sycamore growing out of what had once been a window, "just supposing there are people who use the cellars under all this for any purpose; presumably they could tap these cables and lay on light and heat. And electric cookers, refrigerators, radios, and hair dryers. It would be a help, wouldn't it?"

He took a couple more snaps through gaps in the masonry of the Rathaus, which finished his film. On the following morning he went to a photographer's shop in the Hohestrasse to have it developed and printed and to buy another film. He then walked along the street, wondering whether he would find Spelmann at the Muserkeller, when suddenly hurrying footsteps overtook him and Yeoman's voice saying: "Hambledon! What a stroke of luck. I've been trying to get you at the Gürzenich, but they said that you were out."

"I've been out all the morning. Why? Something happened?"

"Last night, yes. I want to——"

"—tell me about it. Quite right. Look, it's just about lunch time or my stomach's a liar. Let's go to that place where we first met and find a quiet corner."

Yeoman agreed and started off at a pace which Hambledon thought excessive, especially as the thermometer stood in the eighties that day.

"Must you gallop like that?" he said plaintively. "If you really must, by all means let's run, but the Colognites will think there's a fire."

Yeoman apologized and steadied his pace. "There's no hurry, really," he admitted. "It is my mind which is in a turmoil."

Hambledon thought that if he were still like this after something which happened last night the event must have been startling indeed. They entered the restaurant, which was emptying fast, as the usual lunch-hour rush was over. Hambledon led the way to a table in the middle of the room where they could be sure that no one was near enough to overhear them. While the waiter was taking their order and bringing the result Hambledon talked about photography, saying that he wished he were more expert at it since he had been commissioned to write a book called *Cologne Now* and wanted to provide it with photographs specially taken to illustrate the various points which would be emphasized in the letterpress. The waiter retired and George Yeoman said: "Yes, of course. Most invaluable," and waited with his mouth open, ready to go on with his own story as soon as Hambledon gave permission, which he did at once.

"Well? What happened last night?"

"Somebody tried to attack me and got shot instead."

"Did you shoot him?" asked Tommy in the casual tone in which one would ask the time.

"Great Scott, no. I'm not armed, and anyway, there wouldn't have been time, besides——" He stopped to stare at Tommy for a moment and then went on. "It's like this. I've got a room in a second-floor flat in a block which originally faced on the Hohestrasse with shops on the ground floor. Well, now the front is all wrecked, we can't use the front door, of course, so we use the tradesmen's entrance instead. You come down the back stairs and out into a narrow lane which used to run from the Hohestrasse into Ludwigstrasse behind, you get me? It's just an alley, really, and ours is the only door with anything habitable behind it. The other doorways in the alley now are just gaping holes with heaps of rubble inside them. Well, I went home for supper last night and came out again about nine. I was just going to wander round, you know——"

"In spite of the warning note," said Tommy.

"Well, I meant to be careful," said Yeoman in a pained voice. "I went downstairs, out into the alley, and turned towards the Hohestrasse, when suddenly out of a doorway on my left there came the head and shoulders of a man with his right arm raised and something in his hand, looked like a short stick, and all in the same moment there was a sharp crack behind me and the man in the doorway took a step forward and fell headlong right across the path. He had a hole in his head just above the ear."

"Pretty shooting," said Tommy approvingly, "very pretty. That is, if the bullet was meant for your friend with the stick and not for you. Who fired, d'you know?"

"I don't. I just jumped over the body and ran for it into the Hohestrasse."

"Did you recognize the victim?"

"Never saw him before."

"Though presumably he not only knew you but also where you live and something about your habits, such as the fact that you generally go home to supper and come out again afterwards. He also disliked you enthusiastically enough to try to brain you, for which surely you must have given some provocation. Can't you think of anybody you've provoked? No? Then he must have thought you had your pockets bulging with dollars, for I don't believe anybody in Germany today would commit murder for a handful of sterling currency; what would he do with it?"

"But, Mr. Hambledon," protested Yeoman, "this is serious."

"Not nearly so serious as it might have been. Some man didn't like you and is now dead. I call that a cheering thought. Also, somebody likes you well enough to plug your enemy, another cheering thought."

"I don't believe anybody in Cologne likes me well enough for that," said Yeoman unhappily. "Besides, as you said, he might have been trying to shoot me."

"Then you've got one enemy instead of two, which again is encouraging. What did you do after you ran away?"

"Walked in the Dom Square for a couple of hours, keeping in the light. Then I went home and found the police there. They said the dead man had a rubber cosh in his hand. I said I didn't know anything about it."

"You were probably wise and you may be glad to hear that the Cologne police are not very experienced in detection. They mean well but they lack training. What are you going to do? Move somewhere else?"

"Certainly not. I'm not going to be scared off. Besides, the people I'm with are very nice and I've got all the necessary official house papers, you know. No, I'm not moving."

"Attaboy," said Hambledon approvingly. "I shouldn't think that would happen again."

## 6  *HE IS DEAD, MEIN HERR*

Hambledon left Yeoman looking puzzled but reassured and decided to go for a walk to think things over. In spite of his encouraging words he had no doubt that Yeoman had trodden on someone's toes or gone somewhere where he wasn't wanted. Since Yeoman had apparently done little but haunt the neighbourhood of the Unter Goldschmied looking for the girl called Magda, this attack was an additional proof that there was something secret and not at all innocent going on in that area. Hambledon was rather pleased about this; he had felt that there was some interesting activity there long before he had any proof; he had had one of his old "hunches" about it and apparently his hunches were still working. Good. The place must be kept under observation, but not in these clothes; he might as well hope to escape notice if preceded by the town crier riding a zebra and playing "See the Conquering Hero Comes" on a key bugle as when walking about looking so very English. This story about writing a book was going to be useful; any idiocy, Hambledon had noticed, is forgiven to people who write books, and *Cologne Now* was a damned good title. He would have to buy a small notebook and make notes in public. He would——

At this point he was interrupted by Spelmann, who bounced out of a doorway, seized him by the arm, and dragged him inside and up a flight of stairs. The room they entered was Spelmann's office; the door proclaimed his name and profession in Gothic script upon a dazzling brass plate, and the room contained one large desk, four chairs, and walls covered five feet high with filing cabinets.

"Forgive my rude precipitancy," said Spelmann. "From this window I saw you coming, and my delight was such as to make me forget my manners. I have news. Will not the Herr take a seat? I have news."

"Tell me," urged Hambledon, sitting on one chair and throwing his hat upon another, "tell me all."

"These mysteries," said Spelmann, quarter-decking up and down the room with his white hair swirling round his head at each turn, "for there are mysteries within mysteries here, mein Herr, and I shall solve them. I start with the mystery of Karl Torgius and I shall unravel it all. When you get home to your England, even there you will see my name in your papers and you will say to your friends, 'Look at this. When I was in Germany I met that man.' My name will become great, my business will increase, I shall have a real office with clerks in it instead of this converted bedroom. I shall be summoned to Mainz, to Hamburg, to Berlin—but there I shall not go while the Russians sit round it like cats round a mousehole, no! I am, mein Herr, upon the road to fame."

"Heaven make it smooth to you," murmured Hambledon.

"I thank the Herr. I see you coming today just at the moment when I most desire someone before whom to unfold my discoveries. I think of you and there you are, the unbiassed listener, the impartial judge, the detached observer. So!"

"Ach, so," chimed Hambledon solemnly.

"To begin at the beginning. I have had my curiosity aroused by that conglomeration of wreckage, the road called Unter Goldschmied. I keep watch. Indeed, mein Herr, it was not so difficult; one could hide a regiment among those rubble heaps."

"That is quite true," said Tommy Hambledon, once a soldier.

"Those two girls, I cannot make them out. Men go to that area and the girls speak to them. I cannot hear what they say, but some of the men they lead away among the ruins and immediately—but immediately, mein Herr—in a matter of minutes, the girls return without them. That is strange, is it not? One would say that they did but guide the men somewhere and leave them there. One man I saw merely spoke to the girls and passed on alone over the rubble heaps; the Herr has seen the little trodden paths which run here and there? Other men come along and speak to the girls and immediately leave them again as though rebuffed; these men return at once to the inhabited parts of the town. What does the Herr make of that?"

"You have indeed observed well," said Tommy. "I should say that the girls were, as you say, put there to lead certain men, not all men who come, to some place of meeting. There are plenty of cellars beneath those ruins. It suggests some sort of club, does it not? Probably disreputable."

"Disreputable or political."

"Or both."

"Or both, as the Herr so justly says. Well, there is one man who always goes there——"

"One moment," said Hambledon. "How often is this fun fair held? Every night?"

"Oh no. Three nights a week, something like that. Not always the same nights in the week."

"Please go on, I apologize for interrupting you. There is, you say, one man——"

"Who is always there and always rebuffed, or sometimes the girls run away and hide till he has gone away again. He is plainly an Englishman; does the Herr know him?"

"I expect there are quite a number of Englishmen in Cologne for one purpose or another."

"No doubt, no doubt. This one is tall and fair with a small moustache; it is plain that he has been a soldier by his carriage, and he looks always most unhappy." He paused, but Hambledon made no comment and Spelmann went on with his story. "Last night I saw him coming away from that place and I say to myself that I will know where he lives. So I follow him along the Hohestrasse, where he turns into an alley and enters a door. I say to myself that Englishmen being as they are—this is not rude, mein Herr, indeed not, it is a statement founded upon observation—being an Englishman, he will not stay in all the evening; he will, perhaps, have something to eat and thereafter he will certainly come out again. There is an empty doorway in the Hohestrasse just opposite to this alley, so I stand within the doorway and wait."

"Excellent," said Hambledon warmly.

"I wait, and in a very short time there comes along the street a man I know. He is tall and dark and has the bearing of a soldier; his name is Lukas Lotz. He was a lifetime friend of poor Karl Torgius; they were at school together. I find it interesting, mein Herr, when he turns into the alley where the Englishman lives and goes at once into a ruined doorway. As he goes in he is taking something out of his sleeve; it looks like a short stick. I do not bore the Herr?"

"On the contrary," said Hambledon with complete truth, "I am so thrilled I don't know how to sit still."

"Good. He is hardly out of sight when a girl comes along by the way he came and stops close to me to look up the alley. She gets into an angle of brickwork; she was so near me I could have touched her, but she did not see me. I know her; it is the taller of the two girls who haunt the Unter Goldschmied. The dark one."

"Good gracious," said Tommy.

"So we wait, she and I, and a little later Lotz puts his head out of the doorway and immediately draws it back. She saw it, too, for she sighed, mein Herr, I heard it. She walked away from me and I could not see where she went, but a few minutes later I saw her at the far end of the alley. She was taking great care not to be seen, but I saw her, I, Spelmann. My hair is white, but my sight is as keen as ever."

"I think you are a very remarkable man," said Tommy enthusiastically.

"I thank the Herr. She was dressed in grey or brown or a brownish-grey—these colours! Is there one they call fawn?"

"I haven't the faintest idea, but I know what you mean."

"Yes. She blends with her background—doubtless that is why she wears it—and she blends still more when she steps into an angle. She had on a white collar; I could see her doing something to it and it disappeared. When she stood quite still you could not see her, upon my honour. It was not yet dark, but the light was no longer strong, you understand. So we all wait."

"Go on, go on," said Hambledon.

"Presently there comes the sound of a door which opens and shuts and the Englishman steps out in the alley and turns towards me. There is then the girl behind him and Lotz in front, but he does not know about either of them. He is wise or fortunate; he walks down the very middle of the alley. When he has almost reached the empty doorway, Lotz comes forward. I see his head and shoulders and an arm raised with something like a stick in his hand. At precisely that moment, mein Herr, there is a crack like a snapped stick from the far end of the alley and the flash of a gun—or a pistol—a firearm, let us say. Lotz staggers out, falls flat on his face, and does not move. He is dead, mein Herr."

"Pretty shooting," said Tommy for the second time in the same connection, "very pretty shooting. Tell me, what did the Englishman do?"

"He had stopped when he saw Lotz come out; when he fell down the Englishman still looked at him for a moment —a tiny moment—but time seems long in such circumstances, as no doubt the Herr knows. Then he seemed suddenly to come to life. He did not look behind him; he leaped over the body and ran forward, towards me, into the Hohestrasse. Here he had enough self-control to pull up and walk slowly, otherwise someone might have looked to see what made him run, eh?"

"He could not have known where the shot came from," said Tommy. "He might have thought that that also was meant for him."

"He might, indeed, in the upset of the moment, and if I had been in his place," said Spelmann handsomely, "I should have run, too, only I think I would have started that little second earlier. Lotz's body would not have hit the ground before I was round the corner."

"I also," agreed Hambledon. "His—what's the popular phrase?—his reflexes seem to have been a little slow. Perhaps he was lost in thought. What happened next?"

"A passer-by looked up the alley and saw Lotz, went and looked at him, and then came out and found a policeman. I came away, took a little turn round, and came back; by that time there was a crowd. I slipped through and looked at him; there was an entry hole just above the ear. That dark young lady can handle a pistol, indeed she can. A firearm, I should say, until there is more evidence. The thing he was holding was not a stick; it was a rubber cosh, weighted at the end. He might have killed the Englishman."

"Indeed he might," said Hambledon. "I think I know the man you mean. If I see him again I will try to enter into conversation with him. Did you tell the police what you had seen?"

"I? I tell the police? Certainly not. They told me to go away and I obeyed at once. Besides, this is my case. I am sure it is part of my case, the Torgius case upon which I am engaged. It is true that I cannot prove it yet, but I feel it here," said Spelmann, slapping his diaphragm. "Now tell me, what does the Herr think of all this?"

Hambledon paused for a moment's thought. Spelmann was being so extremely helpful and would probably continue to be so, it seemed wise as well as kind to give him a lead.

"It seems to me," he said in grave tones, "that there are two possible reasons why that girl shot Lotz in that alley last night. One is that she meant to shoot him anyway and followed him until she got an opportunity and took it. This implies that the presence of the Englishman was merely coincidental."

"It is possible," said Spelmann, nodding slowly. "Yet I should have thought that in a city like my poor Köln there would be many more convenient places to shoot a man than within twenty yards of the Hohestrasse."

"Yes, but there may have been some urgency of which we know nothing; before he spoke to someone, for example, or went somewhere and saw something it was desirable that he should not see."

"Very true. Very true indeed."

"The other explanation involves the Englishman. There were many English here when Cologne was first captured, were there not? Was he one of them and did he know the dark girl in those days? And, possibly, Lotz too? You may have to go five years back for the clue to the little scene you saw last night, Herr Spelmann."

"I feel," said Spelmann, clasping his inspired diaphragm, "I feel it here that that idea is nearer the truth. The Englishman does not behave like a stranger to Köln."

"You do realize," said Tommy anxiously, "that if that is so, it means that this killing may have no connection at all with the hanging of Karl Torgius?"

Spelmann's lip drooped. "I see that, yes. But," he added, brightening up, "I do not believe it. The Torgius case may not have been the cause of this murder, no. But the same people were involved, I am certain of that. This Lotz, whatever he was doing, Torgius would have been in it too. Lotz led, Torgius followed; that was so always when they were little boys in knickers. I should have talked to Lotz, I see that now, and it is too late. However, it makes no real difference, as he would not have answered. Very arrogant and overbearing always, the Herr Lukas Lotz."

" 'I am the Blessed Glendoveer,' " quoted Hambledon. " ' 'Tis mine to speak and yours to hear.' "

"I never heard of a saint of that name," said Spelmann, "but as regards Lotz, he was like that."

"Reverting to the girl for a moment, you will have no great difficulty in finding out her name, will you?"

"That shall be my first task," said Spelmann.

Hambledon applied a few more well-turned phrases of congratulation and went away, telling himself how lucky he was to have heard both sides of the same story in one day. There was certainly something queer about the Unter Goldschmied, and the girls were probably not what the casual observer would take them to be, but there was still no proof that they had any connection with the Silver Ghosts. Spelmann's description of the girls piloting men through the ruins and coming back at once for more was suggestive of some kind of meeting, but it might quite as easily be a dope party as a political affair. Hambledon knew well enough that in the overcrowded houses of Cologne, where several families lived together, nobody would be able to keep any sort of meeting a secret; mysterious meetings were frowned upon by the Occupying Powers, and rightly. Secrets mean mischief, as a rule.

He reverted to his earlier idea about getting some less conspicuous style of dress and somewhere quiet to change in, not his hotel, definitely not. He strolled along the Hohestrasse and pulled up at Anton's stall. Anton was a young man of rather Jewish appearance who had, indeed, spent a couple of years in a concentration camp for that reason and managed to survive. "They didn't like the shape of my nose," he explained quite frankly. "So they put me inside. Oh, it was not too bad if you knew the ropes. I shall always be a little lame, and my doctor says my heart isn't too good; I shall conk out all of a sudden one day. Still, I'm alive now, ain't I, and the war's over till the next one starts. Sausages!" he cried in a typical barrow boy's voice, raucous with shouting. "Come along, come along! Hot sausage, cold sausage, ice-cold cocoa!"

Hambledon tried the ice-cold cocoa and found it extremely good. The sausages, hot or cold, were served on an oblong cardboard plate with a split roll and a dab of mustard; Anton explained that he could not use china plates because he had no facilities for washing up. "Electric light but no water," he explained. "I bring a bucket of water for cooking, but that's all. Cardboard plates are cheap enough. Come on, ma! Have a sausage, extra-good today!"

Hambledon also had a sausage and it was good, so he had another and started talking to Anton, who proved to be a very pleasant fellow, intelligent and friendly. Hambledon told him about his book, *Cologne Now*, and the difficulties he had in collecting data.

"You see," he said, "I'm an Englishman and look it in

these clothes. People take one look at me and say, 'Ach, tourist!' and dry up. Now my German is quite all right——"

"Your German is darned good," said Anton. "Not too good either, if you get me. Not careful, then. In fact, I'd have taken you for a German if you didn't look so English."

"Well, there you are," said Tommy.

"What you want," said Anton, "is a suit of old clothes. Clean, but shabby, you know, and a peaked cap. Hump your shoulders and slouch along, and there you are."

"Yes, but where could I buy clothes like that?"

"You couldn't, but I could."

"And I should want somewhere to change. My hotel would throw me out on my ear if I came home looking like that."

"You can change behind the stall here. Come inside and look," said Anton. The stall was not a portable barrow but a semi-permanent shed built of timber with match-boarding sides and tar-paper roof; it had a counter along the front and room behind for a small coal-burning cooking stove and two pots, for he boiled his sausages. Anton opened a narrow door in the back of the shop; behind it was a small compartment where he kept his stores. A man could stand up in it quite easily if he did not want to move about; there were even a couple of nails in the wall and Tommy pointed them out.

"I can hang my own clothes up there when I'm wearing the others," he said. "This is fine. Are you sure I'm not giving you too much trouble?"

"Trouble? No trouble at all, pleased to do it. Look, you come back tomorrow evening and I'll have something for you to look at. No need to take them if you don't like."

Hambledon thanked him sincerely and walked away, thinking that the people of Cologne were still just what they used to be, friendly and helpful and always ready to laugh. Any joke produced roars of appreciation, especially if it had a Rabelaisian flavour; the fact that their city was in ruins did not seem to depress them in the least. Things like that must be expected in war, though one man did remark to him in a slightly pained voice that he didn't see why they had to bomb Cologne so much. "Nearly every night, mein Herr, coming or going, they dropped at least some on Cologne, why? Hamburg, yes; Mainz or Berlin, yes, but we are the worst-bombed city in Germany, and why? We are not so important as all that."

Hambledon went home and on the following morning rang up the Dom Hotel to speak to the Herren d'Almeida and Piccione, the Spanish gentlemen, either of them would do. Campbell came, and Hambledon identified himself with some care and then suggested their meeting him for lunch at a restaurant on the other side of the town, up by the Rings. Campbell agreed; Hambledon rang off and was at once called to the telephone again to speak to Yeoman.

## 7  MAGDA VON BERGEN

Yeoman said that he was in a café, which he named, in the Langgasse near the steps, and, though he hated being the nuisance which he undoubtedly was, he would be immensely grateful if he could have the benefit of Hambledon's advice in the critical situation which had arisen. Hambledon said that he would be there in a quarter of an hour, picked up his hat, and went out.

He found Yeoman sitting at a table with a cup of coffee and his luggage, in two kit bags, on the floor at his feet. Hambledon ordered beer because he found it suited him, and remarked that it was odd that German beer should now be stronger than English, whereas before the war it was a lot weaker. "I sometimes wonder who won the war," he added plaintively, "when I think of the beer at home."

Yeoman said it was probably a by-product of the effect of the meridian of longitude upon the precession of the equinoxes. Hambledon blinked, the hovering waiter went hastily away, and Yeoman added that he was only making light conversation.

"Light——" said Tommy blankly. "Oh, I see. Light. Meridian. Noonday. Jolly good. Yes, well, let's abandon that, shall we, for the more urgent question of why you're humping your packed bags round Cologne on so hot a day. Have you been thrown out?"

"They said I must leave at once. They made a variety of excuses, and it was quite obvious that they didn't really want to do it. Throw me out, I mean. They were only doing it because they were afraid. Why, I'd just settled well down into the life of the family, nice people. I'd even found a little place where you could always get fish heads for the cat; they had had considerable difficulty about that."

Hambledon blinked again, but Yeoman was merely looking absently out of the window; a little worried, a little anxious as usual, but perfectly normal. Tommy realized that Yeoman was the type of man who would treat quite seriously the problem of fish heads for the cat, the type that does odd jobs about the house and catches the eight-fifteen every morning with a season ticket; a kindly, faithful soul and a good provider. Tommy's thoughts flew to Magda, the tall girl who walked unafraid, with a step like a deer and her head held high, those awful ruins at dead of night. Lotz had threatened Yeoman, so she shot the German neatly through the head. She must be very fond of Yeoman to do that. Hambledon shook his head impatiently and broke the prolonged silence.

"What are you going to do then? Go away?"

"Of course not," said Yeoman. "I am merely trying to find somewhere else to live, that's all, only it is very difficult. I tried a lot of places near there, but nobody had a room."

"My hotel," began Hambledon.

"Too expensive, I can't afford that."

"Try the Golden Cross," said Tommy. "It's more of a

pub, but they used to let rooms and it's still standing up, I saw it yesterday. Turn left out of this door and left again down towards the Hohestrasse; it's not far. I'll mind your baggage."

Yeoman thanked him and went out while Hambledon talked to the waiter, who came from Bergisch-Gladbach, where his father was killed when the paper mills were bombed. Otherwise the place wasn't much damaged and the Kradepohl was exactly as it used to be, yes, yes, except the little bridge to the island in the lake; fancy the Herr remembering that. It disappeared long ago, nothing to do with the war.

Yeoman came back and the waiter retired modestly. Yeoman said that he had asked if they had a room vacant at the Golden Cross, but the man he had spoken to looked hard at him and said no, definitely no, they were full right up. "I may be mistaken, but I thought he knew me—he looked as though he did—but there was nothing I could do about it. I stood outside for a minute, thinking it over, and another man came to the door with a bag in his hand and asked for a room. They admitted him."

"It looks to me as though the word has gone round against you," said Tommy. "I don't know whose word or why, but there it is."

"I won't go away as long as my money lasts."

"No, of course not, but you'll have to go further afield. Why don't you take the tram across the Neue Brücke to Köln-Deutz and look for something there? I shouldn't think they'd have heard of you over there, and it might—I don't know, but it might be cheaper."

"Thank you so very much. I was sure you would suggest

something. You know," said Yeoman, standing up and lighting a cigarette before leaving, "I've never been the sort of man to cope with emergencies, not all on my own, I mean. In the Army there was always someone to tell you what to do and you did it. You must find me a frightful nuisance, but may I let you know how I get on?"

"Please do," said Hambledon. "Ring me up and we'll arrange to meet, tomorrow if you like. I've got rather a lot on hand today. I do hope you'll find somewhere suitable."

"Oh, I expect so," said Yeoman, picking up his bags. "I don't want much. Only a clean small room, you know." He drifted out of the café, and Hambledon saw him pass the windows on his way down the street.

"Magda," said Hambledon thoughtfully. "Magda, it must be your maternal instinct working overtime. I should think they'd be very happy."

The waiter saw his lips move and came up to the table.

"Tell me," said Hambledon earnestly, "what is it that makes people marry the people they do marry?"

The waiter smiled. "God knows, as they say, but I think even the good God must occasionally be surprised."

Hambledon looked at his watch and decided that there was plenty of time, before his lunch engagement with Forgan and Campbell, to go to Spelmann's office and see if he had any fresh news. He went, therefore, and found Spelmann on the point of going out.

"I do not want to detain you; indeed I have an engagement myself," began Tommy. "I only wondered whether there was any news about your case."

Spelmann's face lit up; he drew Hambledon into the office and shut the door behind them.

"I have made progress," he said, "distinct progress. The name of the dark girl who shot Lotz is Magda von Bergen, and she lives in an apartment house at the top of the Schildergasse, just before you come to the Neumarkt. She is a girl of good family; the apartment house is quite all right, you understand, clean and well conducted, but not such as the Fräulein von Bergen was formerly used to. That was my last night's work; early this morning I came here to my office and looked for the name Von Bergen in a pre-war *Directory and Street Guide to Cologne.* I found the name; there was a Herr Doktor August-Wilhelm von Bergen who had a house outside Cologne on the Thielenbrück road. Her father, perhaps? I took a tram and went there. It is a nice house standing in its own grounds, a big house with a drive entrance and a lodge at the gates. I went to the lodge and asked if the *hochgeboren* Herr Doktor von Bergen still lived there. The woman who opened the door was very old but most respectable, the type of the faithful family servant, you know?"

"I used to," said Tommy Hambledon, remembering his own nurse in a country rectory in England. "Never mind. I know what you mean, go on."

"She said that the *gnädiger* Herr Doktor had died in 1947 and that the *gnädige* Frau Ottilie von Bergen had died during the war, so as the sons were both married and lived elsewhere, the house was sold to a rich building contractor, 'on condition,' she said, 'that I am allowed to live here rent-free for the rest of my life. The house was too big, you understand, for the *gnädiges* Fräulein Magda to live here alone.' Then I knew, Herr Hambledon, that I had rung the right bell."

"You were lucky to do so at the first attempt."

"It is true that they were the only Von Bergens in the directory," said Spelmann. "I said that the house was indeed large—you could see it from the lodge—it must have been inconveniently large for the Herr Doktor, his wife, and one daughter. The woman said that that was so, but that as soon as the invading armies reached Cologne foreign officers were billeted there. I said yes, I had heard that; in fact, that was what had brought me there. My son, I said— I have no son, mein Herr, but I have invented him so often that I almost believe in him—my son had received a great kindness from an English officer billeted there and, wishing to write to him, had asked me to come and try to find out his present address. A Captain Stuart, I said—that is an English name, is it not?"

"Well, in a way, yes," said Tommy, who did not feel called upon to explain the exact relationship between Scotland and England. "There are a lot of Stuarts in England, anyway."

"She said there was no officer of that name there, was I sure I had it right? I said I was by no means sure, and that was heaven's own truth, as the Herr knows. She then told me several names which I wrote down as soon as I was out of sight. Barkley. Hitchcock. Burns. Van Buren, an American. Yeoman. Wilson, and Hopkiss, another American. When the Herr came I was about to set out for the house where Fräulein von Bergen's Englishman lives to find out if he bears any of those names."

"Save yourself the trouble," said Hambledon. "His name is Yeoman."

"Ah! You have spoken to him?"

"I met him in a café this morning; we got talking and he asked my advice. He does not live there any more, Herr Spelmann; he was turned out. What is more, at whatever place in this district he asks for a room he is told they are full up," said Hambledon significantly.

Spelmann walked up and down the room. "The order has gone out that he is not to be accommodated?"

"I think so——"

"Do not tell me he is gone back to England!"

"No. I suggested that he should try across the river at Köln-Deutz. I should think he would get in there somewhere. They cannot rule the whole of Cologne and all its suburbs, whoever 'they' may be. He is going to let me know. He is very lonely here."

"Poor man. I would like to speak to him, I——"

"No use, he doesn't know as much as we do. He came back here to see the Fräulein von Bergen, but she won't have anything to do with him."

"And yet she shot that Lotz——"

"Precisely," said Hambledon.

"Having followed him from wherever he came from. Then she knew what was going to happen?"

"Presumably."

"So I was right, Lukas Lotz was mixed up in whatever is going on in the Unter Goldschmied."

"Not necessarily. It may have been just plain jealousy which made him attack Yeoman. Human nature, Herr Spelmann, remember human nature. The *gnädiges* Fräulein is a very attractive young woman."

"The Herr has an exact and logical mind," said Spelmann gloomily.

94

Hambledon looked at his watch and sprang to his feet. "Good heavens, I must go, I have a luncheon appointment. Shall I see you this evening?"

"At the Muserkeller," said Spelmann, hurrying round to open the door for him, "at about nineteen hours or a little after?"

"A little after," said Tommy, running down the stairs. "Auf Wiedersehen."

He found Forgan and Campbell waiting for him at the appointed place. It was fairly full, so they put off talking business until after lunch. They lingered over the meal until the company in the restaurant began to thin out. Forgan leaned back and patted his waistcoat.

"You know," he said thoughtfully, "I like German cooking."

"You do feel you've had something," agreed Campbell.

"The Germans have one great advantage over English kitchens; they've got something to cook," said Tommy. "I know it's dear, but they can get it."

"Let's forget the meat ration," said Forgan firmly.

"You could, easily," said Campbell acidly.

"Hush," said Tommy. "Any news?"

"We've had a letter," said Forgan, and gave it to Hambledon. It was typed on plain white paper and bore no date or address.

> If the distinguished Herren d'Almeida and Piccione will be so courteously obliging as to remain within their hotel during tomorrow morning, there is one who will do himself the singular honour of calling upon them to discuss oranges.

"Unsigned," commented Tommy, and handed it back.

"Very dignified, isn't it?" said Forgan. "Very stately."

"Comes down with a bit of a bump at the end, don't you think?" said Campbell. "All that, and then 'to discuss oranges.' He should have put 'for the purpose of entering into mutual discussion about the law of supply and demand as applicable to citrus fruit.' "

" 'Vitamin-starved populations, for the comfort of,' " suggested Tommy. "You know, I think your caller, whoever he is, might well be looked over by a trained observer who might even recognize him with any luck, and thereafter be followed home."

"Why?" said Campbell. "Do you think you know who's coming?"

"Oh no," said Hambledon. "The trained observer won't be me. I have a private detective."

The two modelmakers looked at each other. "What does he mean," said Forgan, " 'I have a private detective'? They aren't things you have. You employ them or hear of them or shun them or even know one of them if your tastes are sufficiently mixed, but you don't have them. You might as well say you have an eclipse of the moon."

"I knew a man once who had a Tierra del Fuegian," said Campbell. "She was his aunt."

"Did she live at Tunbridge Wells?" asked Forgan.

"No, why? She lived in a lighthouse."

"I'll buy it," said Hambledon. "Why did she live in a lighthouse?"

"Because she was a Tierra del Fuegian, of course. Now tell us about your private detective."

"Tierra del—— Of course," said Tommy. "Land of Fire. I suppose they used her instead of a lamp."

"She drank methylated spirits. The detective——"

"He has a card; I've got one," said Hambledon. "Here it is." He tossed it across the table and went on: "I didn't say I employed him because I don't pay him; in a sense he employs me, though it is true he doesn't pay me either. I certainly don't shun him because I think he's going to be useful, but I do know him quite well. He uses me as a sort of test tube to try out his ideas in. He thinks I am just a casual English tourist with no local knowledge and therefore a completely impartial observer."

"I like 'discretion and despatch,' " said Forgan, handing the card back.

"I told you when we first met that I had come across some funny business but I didn't think it had anything to do with what we're looking for," said Hambledon. "Now I'm not so sure. Listen," and he told them the whole story of the odd happenings in the Unter Goldschmied, starting with the hanging of Karl Torgius which was, in some respects, so unlike a suicide. He described the two girls, especially Magda von Bergen, included Spelmann's account of the shooting of Lukas Lotz, and finished with George Yeoman looking for a room to let. He ended by saying, as he had said to Spelmann, that the meetings might be some sort of vice racket and Lotz's attack on Yeoman merely jealousy. "But it might be something else."

"We looked at that area this morning," said Forgan. "We went down the Grosse Budengasse as far as the road you mention, but it had no name so far as we could see. It has one street lamp on a pole, but I don't suppose it works."

"Oh yes, it does," said Hambledon, and told them about the electric cables. "It's just around that light that the girls are usually seen. Spelmann said at first that they were 'miserable girls who frolic among the ruins'; they may be miserable, but I think there is something a little unusual about their frolics."

"We didn't go any further than that corner," said Campbell. "It didn't look very attractive and our feet hurt. I wouldn't like to drive a car down those roads."

"It looks the sort of place which would naturally attract ghosts," said Forgan. "Especially silver ones."

Hambledon nodded and said he would tell Spelmann to have a look at whoever should come to the Dom Hotel to see them the next morning. They agreed at once.

"I take it you haven't told him what you're after?"

"I have not," said Tommy. "I rather doubt if his weight is up to that contest. He will be useful, I'm sure, but he'd better not know too much. I'll tell him some yarn about your visitor."

"Tell him he's a justly enraged husband," said Forgan.

"Tell him he's blackmailing us," said Campbell. "We were young once, believe it or not."

"I don't think you're much older now," said Tommy.

He met Spelmann at the Muserkeller as arranged and asked him to have a look at a man who would be calling at the Dom Hotel to see the Señores d'Almeida and Piccione. "I know them," said Tommy; "we met in Spain. They are not experienced travellers; this is their first visit to Germany. They are fruit exporters and have come here to sell oranges. Their visitor may be quite all right, but he has no introduction of any kind and they are a bit—you know——"

"A little apprehensive," said Spelmann, nodding his head. "A little nervous in a strange land; it is natural, it is to be

98

expected. How kind you are to protect them like this. Have no fear, Herr Hambledon, I will spread my wings over your poor innocents."

Hambledon choked violently, apologized, and said his beer must have gone down the wrong way.

At about nine o'clock that night an elderly labourer emerged from behind Anton's stall. He wore heavy boots much patched, shabby working clothes, a cap with a shiny peak, and steel-rimmed spectacles. He walked with a tired slouch, his shoulders were bent with a lifetime of labour, and he carried a black American cloth bag with not much in it. He went up the Hohestrasse away from the Cathedral; turned left into Gürzenichstrasse, keeping on the side opposite the hotel, and turned left again into the ruins. At one time there was a road through here which became the Unter Goldschmied further on; now it is not easy to see even where it used to run, as the area is much encumbered with barricades, wooden hoardings, bulldozer excavations, and other preliminaries to rebuilding. There is a wandering track through here for those who know where to go, and the labourer plodded on, stopping several times to relight his pipe, which kept on going out. Hambledon was never a pipe smoker. He went steadily but slowly on down the whole length of the Unter Goldschmied, not looking about him but keeping his eyes on the road, which was, indeed, rough enough to need it. He saw no one and heard nothing. Nearly an hour later he went back again down the Grosse Budengasse, along the Unter Goldschmied, and out eventually into the Gürzenichstrasse as he had come; his bag was fuller and heavier now. No one was about and nobody challenged him.

"Not one of their nights," he said to himself, and went back to Anton's stall to change into his English tweeds.

"How did you get on?" asked Anton.

"Oh, much better. People talk quite differently to a poor old man like me. May I do this again tomorrow night if it isn't troubling you?"

"Do it every night for a month and welcome. It's no trouble to me."

"I shouldn't think it would take so long as a month," said Tommy Hambledon.

## 8 *LIGHT FOR A CIGARETTE*

On the following morning Heinrich Spelmann, private investigator, went to the Dom Hotel and explained to the reception clerk that he had come there to meet a friend but had mislaid the card which told him what time his friend was arriving. He would sit in the hall and wait if it would not be an inconvenience? Even if it were for an hour or more? Splendid. Most kind.

He sat down in an inconspicuous place within earshot of the reception desk and waited. Time passed by, so did people. Spelmann marvelled, not for the first time, upon the variety of questions which travellers ask and how extraordinarily seldom reception clerks are stumped for an answer. At the end of an hour and ten minutes a neat inconspicuous man came up to the desk and asked if the Herren d'Almeida and Piccione were in the hotel, the Spanish gentlemen.

The clerk said that he had not seen them go out but would ring up their room to make sure. What name, please?

He said that his own name would convey nothing to the gentlemen; he was representing the firm of So-and-so, mentioning a genuine wholesale fruit business in Cologne. "They are expecting a call from us," he added.

The clerk nodded, turned to the house telephones, and rang up a number. While he was talking the visitor, leaning one elbow on the desk, looked casually at a leaflet advertising steamer trips up the Rhine. Almost behind him on a chair against the wall Spelmann rather drooped than sat with the air of one who has already waited much too long and has passed through impatience to resignation. He gazed absently out through the revolving doors at the sunlit square outside and took no interest in anybody.

The clerk said that the Spanish gentlemen were in their room and would be happy to receive their visitor. The man nodded, walked across to the lift, and was taken up out of sight. Spelmann uncrossed his legs, crossed them over the other way, sighed deeply, and lit a cigarette.

"Your friend is long in coming," said the clerk in a friendly tone.

"I shall not wait much longer," said Spelmann gloomily.

"Since you have lost his letter, are you sure that this is the right day?"

"Yes," said Spelmann. "Quite, at least, almost sure." He allowed a note of doubt to creep into his voice. "I shall wait a little longer," he said.

Five minutes later the lift came down bringing Forgan, Campbell, and their visitor; they walked together across the hall without speaking and curvetted seriatim through the revolving doors.

Spelmann lost patience suddenly and exclaiming: "Ach! I cannot wait any longer!" got up and also went out into the square. Forgan, Campbell, and their escort were about twenty yards ahead, going straight across the square, threading their way between the parked cars. Spelmann followed more deviously, seeing as he went the patient figure of Tommy Hambledon absorbing beer at the Muserkeller. The three men in front walked straight across without hesitation and entered the pillared portals of the Excelsior Hotel opposite.

Spelmann waited for a few minutes, strolled in after them, and ordered a cup of coffee at a table which commanded the entrance hall. Neither Forgan, Campbell, nor their visitor was in sight, but almost at once the visitor came into the hall, sat down at a table, and also ordered coffee. It had hardly been served when a tall young man with a hard face and a particularly square jaw came in from the street and in passing glanced casually at the visitor, who tilted his head very slightly; if Spelmann had not been watching closely he would not have seen it. The young man made no sign at all and walked through with long strides towards the lift. Forgan's visitor drank off his coffee and quite deliberately went out into the street. Spelmann stayed where he was.

Ten minutes later Forgan and Campbell, unescorted, passed through the hall and out into the sunshine. The detective waited for some time but saw no more of the young man with the square jaw.

Spelmann went across the square and found Hambledon still patiently waiting at the Muserkeller and discussing cameras with the Cologne official photographer who had taken his photograph shortly after his arrival. Spelmann, being among friends, was greeted with cries of "Herr Holmes" and asked if he had yet discovered who stole the cat's fish head on Trinity Sunday.

The place emptied as its customers went back to their afternoon's work, and the little table at which Hambledon and Spelmann sat became sufficiently isolated for private conversation. Tommy leaned across the table and said, "Well?"

Spelmann described what had happened and added that he knew the man who had asked for Forgan and Campbell at the Dom Hotel. "He is Hugo Geisel; his father is a paper-maker with several factories in the district. He had a house in Cologne, but it was destroyed; I don't know where he is living now. It was quite obvious that Geisel merely conducted your friends to a room upstairs at the Excelsior, and of course I cannot say whom they saw there. They will no doubt tell you."

"Yes," said Hambledon, "yes. But the Herr Hugo Geisel does not deal in fruit?"

"Certainly not. He is with his father in the paper business, which he will no doubt inherit in due course. They have plenty of money and this young man is no rake. He would be no party to anything like a confidence trick, if that is what your friends are fearing. He was always regarded as definitely serious. On the other hand——"

Spelmann stopped and Hambledon waited, but no more came, so he prompted gently: "On the other hand?"

"The Herr will say that I have my mysteries on the brain," said the detective energetically. "Nevertheless, there is a connection. Before the war there was a gang of young men—no, not a gang, for they were all well bred and well behaved. A clique is more genteel, is it not? A group?"

"A group, let us say," said Tommy.

"A group of young men in our city all much of an age, having gone to the same school and belonging to the same social class, who did everything together; it is quite usual, is it not? They had a rowing club on the Rhine, they organized shooting parties together, they went to Switzerland for the winter sports. Karl Torgius was one, Lukas Lotz another, Hugo Geisel was another. So was the elder of Fräulein Magda von Bergen's brothers while he lived here. I suppose there were fifteen or twenty, more or less; some moved away from Köln, and so on. Most of them were killed in the war, of course, but there are left those I have mentioned, and I saw another this morning, Gustav Volkenborn. He came into the Excelsior soon after your friends did and passed through the hall; I didn't see him come out again. There is no reason why he shouldn't be there, of course, but I did think it odd that he didn't stop and speak to Geisel."

"Perhaps they've quarrelled."

"I thought that Geisel made him a small sign, a slight jerk of the head, and Volkenborn did not smile, but he looked as though he had been told something—the Herr knows that look?"

"Quite unmistakable," agreed Tommy.

"I therefore wondered in my mind whether by chance it were he who was going to meet your friends. I lay my mind open to you, I have no proof. Only, if it were Gustav Volkenborn, again there is no cheap trickery involved."

"Describe him," said Tommy, and Spelmann did so.

"I will ask my friends," went on Hambledon, "whether that was the man, and no doubt they will also tell me what he had to say. I take it the Herr Volkenborn doesn't deal in fruit either?"

"Certainly not, except perhaps as cargo. His father was a shipowner, river boats on the Rhine, cargo, not passenger.

He died last year, and this young man is now the Volken-born Rheinische Schiffahrtsgesellschaft—the Rhine Shipping Company."

"I see," said Hambledon thoughtfully. "Well, I think I'll stand myself some lunch somewhere and then see if my friends are at home. I'd like to hear what they have to say."

About an hour later Hambledon rang up the Dom Hotel and spoke to Forgan.

"Do you feel like seeing a little of the beauties of the countryside this afternoon?"

"Beauties of all kinds," said Forgan, "always appeal to our better selves."

"Do you know where the Neue Brücke is? . . . Yes, it goes across the river, you're quite right. . . . Oh, you do know it, good. Well, if you'll go there you'll find a tram stop just this side of the bridge from whence the trams go every half-hour or so to a place called Schlodderdich. If you'll take the first tram after three o'clock I shall be in the rear compartment. You will be up in front somewhere. O.K.? . . . Good."

Three men, among other passengers, left the tram at Schlodderdich; one of them started to walk across the fields towards Bergisch-Gladbach, the other two followed after. When the first man stopped to admire the view the other two naturally caught him up.

"I think we did that very naturally," said Forgan. "Tell me, what is a Schlodderdich? Campbell thinks it's a plate of tripe."

"How did you get on this morning?" asked Hambledon.

"Oh, quite well. One man called for us and led us to the other tavern opposite, where we were taken up to a room on the first floor and asked to wait. Our guide went away and a few minutes later another man came instead. All he did was to apologize for the delay in calling upon us; there was someone very important indeed—his voice dropped when this was said—coming from a long distance to meet us, and unexpected difficulties had forced him to put off his visit for a few days. He hoped that we were comfortable and not too bored. He begged in a haughty voice that we would forgive the apparent discourtesy; he would let us know at the earliest possible moment when the meeting would be held, and in the meantime the resources of Cologne, such as they were, were at our service for interest and entertainment. He then said '*Auf Wiedersehen*' to each of us, with a bow each thrown in, and left the room. We didn't say one word from start to finish."

"It must have been a very short interview," said Tommy.

"It was. We weren't sure whether we were supposed to wait for the first man to come back or not, so we hung about for a few minutes and then came away. That's all."

"Will you describe the man you met upstairs?"

They did so, and Hambledon said: "The Herr Gustav Volkenborn, owner of the Volkenborn Rheinische Schiffahrtsgesellschaft."

"And the other man?"

"The Herr Hugo Geisel. His father makes paper."

"Wonderful how he does it, isn't it?" said Forgan to Campbell.

"He was, of course," said Campbell, "the housemaid who was polishing the corridor; didn't you see her?"

"What," said Forgan, "the one with the harelip?"

"No, no," said Campbell, horrified, "the one with the squint."

"You're both wrong," said Hambledon. "I was the second potted palm on the left of the lift. Listen," and he told them what Spelmann had said.

"A handy nucleus for a secret society," said Forgan.

"Karl Torgius," said Campbell. "Wasn't that the fellow who was found hanged?"

"Yes," said Hambledon. "That reminds me——"

"What?"

"Only something I must ask Spelmann."

"Was he the white-haired gink sitting in the Dom hall looking as though he were collecting evidence for a divorce?"

"For heaven's sake," said Hambledon, "don't make such a suggestion to him, he'd be most insulted. I gather he left that sort of thing behind him on the lower rungs of the ladder long ago."

Much later that evening the elderly and scruffy labourer once more plodded heavily up the Hohestrasse from Anton's stall, made a circuit near the Gürzenich, and came along the Unter Goldschmied; this time he saw the two girls standing at the corner of the Laurenzplatz. He took not the faintest notice of them, and though they looked at him they did not speak. When he came back the same way a little after ten they were loitering about under the solitary street light in the Unter Goldschmied. Hambledon came steadily up the road towards them, clumping noisily in his heavy boots; just before he reached them he stopped for a moment to relight his pipe. His bag revealed a large purple pickling cabbage. When he came abreast of the girls they ran into the road and spoke to him.

"Hullo, daddy! Give us a light for our cigarettes."

"Huh?" said Hambledon, turning his left ear towards them.

The fair girl came a pace nearer and lifted her voice. "Be a nice daddy and give us a light for our cigarettes."

"No business to be smoking, young girls like you," growled Hambledon. "Don't know what your mothers are about to let you do it." He made no move to go on but merely stood staring owlishly at them with red-rimmed eyes behind the steel spectacles. He also smelt of beer.

"Oh, don't be a pig," said the fair girl imploringly. "We haven't had a smoke for hours an' hours an' hours; you know what that's like, you're smoking. Just one little match, daddy dear."

"Don't you call me 'daddy dear,'" grumbled Tommy in his deepest voice. "If I was your daddy you wouldn't be about 'ere this time o' night. Ought to be ashamed of yourselves." However, he fumbled in the pockets of his ancient coat and slowly drew out a box of matches. "Suppose if I don't give you a light some other fool will."

He struck one match, broke it, dropped the pieces, and complained that they had made him waste one. The second attempt was successful, and he held out the flaring match in a hand sufficiently unsteady to make them pursue, as it were, the flame with the ends of their cigarettes. He had a very good view of their faces.

"Where are you going to, daddy?" asked Magda von Bergen, speaking for the first time.

"'Ome. Same as you ought to be doin'."

"Oh, don't be so grumpy, daddy," said the fair girl. "I'm sure you're a nice old daddy really."

"Garrh! Hussy!"

"I haven't seen you about here before, have I?" said Magda.

"No. 'Cause I didn't live 'bout 'ere before, that's why. Come to that, what're you doin' 'bout 'ere?"

"We came here in the hope of meeting you, daddy darling, of course," said the fair girl.

Hambledon emitted a high-pitched cackle of senile laughter and plodded on along the road without farewell of any kind. His ears were quick and he was moving slowly; he caught the girls' comments plainly enough.

"Harmless," said Magda, "quite harmless."

"Goofy, if you ask me," said the other.

"By the time I've done this for a week," said Hambledon to himself, "they'll take no more notice of me than they do of that lamppost of theirs."

He had just finished lunch next day when a message was brought to him that the Herr Winklebottom was on the telephone for him.

"Who—oh, yes, I know," said Hambledon, and went to the office. "Hullo, that you, Winklebottom?"

"That you, Hambledon?" said Forgan's voice. "We are examining the ruins of the Rathaus this afternoon. We thought it would be much more interesting if you could come along and tell us what it used to be like."

"Certainly. When are you starting? . . . At once. Good-bye."

He slung his camera from his shoulder and went by a circuit to the towering ruin; long before he got there he saw two figures wandering round it, tumbling knee-deep in weeds.

"We have some things to show you," said Forgan, "and we thought we might be private here. Campbell?"

"Look what I won," said Campbell, and showed him a studio photograph of a British officer in uniform. "Do you happen to know who it is?"

"Of course," said Hambledon instantly. "That's George Yeoman; I told you about him, didn't I? Where did you get that?" Across the corner was written: "Magda with love from George."

"At the same place where we got this," said Forgan, and gave him a .32 automatic pistol which had been fired fairly recently, for the gun had not been cleaned since.

"We made the acquaintance last night of the gracious Fräulein Magda von Bergen and her blond pal. When I say 'made their acquaintance,' it didn't flourish," said Forgan. "Fearing lest we might have been thought rude, we decided to call on her to apologize, but she was out."

"The concierge, whatever that is in German, said she was in," said Campbell, "so we went upstairs. She lives on the second floor."

"But——" said Hambledon.

"You gave us the address, didn't you? We thought you meant us to make use of it."

"Actually," said Forgan, "we thought that the concierge must be mistaken because we could have sworn we saw her walking away just before we got to the door."

"So we went upstairs," added Campbell, "and when there was no reply to our discreet tapping on the door, we went in."

"Wasn't it locked?" asked Tommy.

"Was it locked, Campbell?" asked Forgan. "I don't remember much about it."

"I myself am not too clear," said the redheaded man.

"There was a little momentary difficulty, was there not?"

"You are a pair of hell-hounds," said Tommy with conviction.

"So we went in but we couldn't find her, although we looked under the bed and in the drawers and a few odd places like that. So we came away again almost at once."

"But why bring the photograph?"

"Merely to prove to you that we'd been to the right place," said Forgan. "She won't miss it at once; it was underneath a pile of what I believe is called lingerie."

"About this gun," said Hambledon. "If we fired another shot out of it a ballistics expert would be able to tell whether it was the same gun which fired the shot——"

"Which delivered the Herr Lotz to the company of his ancestors," said Campbell. "Exactly. Do you want that proved?"

"My education was in some respects deficient," said Forgan. "I never learned Greek. So on our way here I bought a Liddell and Scott's *Lexicon* from a stall. It is a nice fat book for fifty pfennigs, ain't it?"

"It would be a pity to waste the chance after all the trouble you've taken," said Hambledon. "If we found a cellar that didn't look too dangerous——"

They found one attainable by a scramble, and Forgan said he hoped the shot wouldn't bring the ceiling down.

"Reinforced concrete," said Hambledon. "If the bombing didn't bring it down, this won't. Will you keep a lookout, Campbell? Though there's never anyone about here bar a few courting couples sometimes. Stand the book up on that lump outside there, will you? I think I can hit that from here."

Campbell climbed out again, put the book up as directed, and a moment later called: "All clear." There was a sharp crack, blue smoke drifted across the cellar, and the book sprang into the air and fell down flat. Hambledon and Forgan scrambled out into the air, and Forgan said that that was better. There was an odd smell, he said, in that cellar.

"The weather's been hot," said Hambledon. Forgan looked at him, turned a little green, and did not pursue the subject. Tommy picked up the book; the bullet had stopped just short of the further cover.

"I doubt, really, whether Spelmann has got a ballistics expert on tap," he said. "I think he's a little new to murder, but there's the evidence if we want it. Now, I'm terribly sorry to bother you, but these souvenirs have got to be returned. I hope you don't think I'm not appreciative, but——"

"Oh, that's all right. I told Campbell you might say that. We'll stroll along there presently."

"Ring me up at the Gürzenich," said Tommy, "the moment you have any news. Say that my films have been developed and will I call for them. I'll meet you——"

" 'Come where the beer is cheapest,' " quoted Forgan. "We found a Café Bensburg—where was it——"

"I know," said Hambledon, "but it isn't cheap."

"Never mind," said Campbell, "the British Government can run to it. Look what they pay for peanuts. Shall we go and see if the lady has come home yet, Forgan?"

"I shall not know tranquillity," said Forgan, getting up from the fallen lintel upon which he had been sitting, "until last night's little misunderstanding has been put right. Aren't these stones hard?"

"If I'm not being tactless," said Hambledon curiously, "what was the misunderstanding?"

"I'm not quite sure," said Campbell; "our German, you know, is so bad, and they didn't speak Spanish."

"We rather gathered," said Forgan, "that they thought we wanted to buy a diamond necklace. Or the Hohenzollern Bridge."

"Sophie was definitely rude," added Campbell.

"She's the fair one, is she?"

"But not at all fair to us. Come on, Forgan."

## 9  THE HOODED MEN

When Forgan and Campbell reached the apartment house where Magda lived the concierge recognized them as that morning's visitors and said that they were unlucky this time, the Fräulein von Bergen was out.

"We can wait a little?" said Forgan.

"By all means, gentlemen. There is, upon each landing, a seat provided for those who wish to wait."

"Shall we go up, then?" said Forgan to Campbell, and Campbell said: "*Jawohl.*" They walked quietly up the two flights—there was no lift—and went straight to Magda's door. Forgan tried the handle while Campbell felt in his pocket for a small instrument which he had used earlier, but it was not necessary. The door opened at once, and Magda von Bergen turned from the window to confront them.

There was nothing else for it; they walked straight in and shut the door behind them.

"Who are you?" she said angrily. "How dare you come into my room?"

"Because we wanted to see you, Fräulein," said Forgan in his atrocious German. "We called this morning, but you were out."

"You were the man last night—— Get out or I will ring the bell for——"

"Let us introduce ourselves," said Forgan, "for last night you had a friend with you and I was not sure who she was. I have the honour to be Miguel Piccione, a gentleman of Spain, entirely at your service, and this is the hidalgo Alfonso Demetrio d'Almeida, also your servant."

She stared them down. "These names mean nothing to me. Once more, will you go before I have you thrown out?"

"I should not ring that bell, señorita," said Campbell. "I beg pardon, I should have said *gnädiges* Fräulein, should I not? There is a little matter of a shooting, is there not?"

She stiffened but did not answer.

"I think," went on Campbell, "that you would not wish the police to hear about that, would you?" Out of the tail of his eye he saw Forgan, who had crossed the room, slip the photograph under the cover on the bedside table. "Correct me if I am wrong, but I think your organization would hardly approve of that either, would they? While on that subject, Fräulein, so excellent a shot as you are should know better than to leave a gun dirty after having been fired. We had to clean it for you." He drew it out of his pocket and, since she made no move to take it, laid it down upon the chest of drawers.

"The Fräulein will realize," said Forgan, "that we are busy men who have come a long journey to speak with someone you know. We have been here several days now and we are not accustomed to being kept waiting."

"But," she said, "you were——" and stopped.

"So you do know about it, Fräulein. I will ask you to be so good as to tell your organization that it is not we, D'Almeida and Piccione, who are suppliants for money. We should also like to know by whose orders our rooms were

entered and our suitcases broken into. I will not swear in
the presence of a lady, but I will ask you, is this the way to
treat a beneficent friend?"

"Say what you have to say," she said, "and go."

"In a word, then," said Campbell, "tell your friends to
hold this meeting quickly, or we return to Spain."

"And as for your childish performance last night," said
Forgan, "if you cannot do better than that, you have no
place in a concern of this importance."

"Señorita," said Campbell, "I have the honour to wish
you a very good day." He bowed deeply and opened the
door.

"Fräulein," said Forgan with another bow, "I kiss your
hands and feet," which is a formal Spanish leave-taking and
is not, normally, impertinent. They both went out, shutting the door behind them, walked down the stairs, out of
the house, and some distance away before either of them
uttered a word.

"Wonder what our Tommy'll say to that?" said Forgan.

"Well, we bolted his rabbit for him, didn't we?"

When Hambledon was told about this, all he said was:
"If I were you I'd keep well away from the Rhine quays,
especially at night."

"Why—oh, you're thinking of our friend the What's-it
Shipping Company. Volkenborn, was it?"

"You don't want to end up exploring the bottom of the
Rhine with weights tied to your feet, do you?"

He rang up Spelmann and said: "The first young man
who was found hanged in the Unter Goldschmied, you remember telling me about him?"

"Kahn," said Spelmann's voice, "Franz Kahn. Yes, what
about him?"

"Was he also a member of that clique or group we were talking about the other day?"

There was a short pause. "He was," said Spelmann. "Not a very early member—he was younger than the others—but he has been about with them since the war was over."

"He was younger than the others," repeated Hambledon evenly. "Any more news?"

"Not yet, mein Herr."

By the first post next morning Campbell had a second letter; like the first, it was unsigned and bore no address:

> The meeting which the distinguished Herren d'Almeida and Piccione are requested to honour with their company will be held in the evening of Thursday. Fuller particulars regarding time and place will reach the Herren tomorrow. It is hoped that they will forgive a reminder to bring with them the documents already agreed upon.

"When they say 'the documents already agreed upon,'" said Forgan, "do they mean some definite documents which have already been discussed and approved, or merely certain specified evidences of our identity?"

"Such as a passport," added Campbell, "a birth certificate, a matriculation certificate, a vaccination scar, a badge of the Primrose League, and a membership card of the Ancient Order of Druids?"

"I shouldn't worry," said Hambledon. "If they have asked for fancy evidences of identity you will have them in the Spaniards' luggage, won't you? If it's some special document you can just turn haughty and say you wouldn't think of producing stuff like that until you have some evidence of identity from them."

"Dammit, sir," said Campbell with a sweeping gesture, "you haven't even got the guts to sign your letters!"

"That's the stuff," said Tommy. " 'Be bloody, bold, and resolute.' By the way, you're D'Almeida, aren't you, Campbell? And Forgan is Piccione?"

"That's right," said Forgan. "It's a question of height, you see. D'Almeida was the tall one, and we thought we'd better match, as it were. A question of clothes, largely."

"I didn't see them, of course," said Hambledon. "By the way, how long does it take a slow cargo boat to reach Buenos Aires from France?"

"Oh, seven or eight weeks at least, then they've got to get themselves out of that mess and travel home again. We've got plenty of time," said Campbell.

Next morning brought them another letter, but this time the envelope merely contained a small street map of Cologne apparently cut out of a guide. Upon it was marked in red ink a route starting from the Dom Square, going along the Marzellenstrasse, turning up past the church of St. Ursula and her eleven thousand virgins, and thence turning about in an aimless pattern of small streets and squares. Across the bottom of the map was written: "Please start walking at a quarter to twenty-one hours; you will be met en route."

"Well, that's all right," said Hambledon, busy taking notes. "I'll be there or thereabouts."

But when the evening came it was anything but all right. Black clouds gathered over Cologne, the night came in early and oppressively hot, and at frequent intervals the rain fell in torrents. Campbell and Forgan, perspiring freely in waterproofs, tramped the streaming streets along their line of route until there was no need to simulate ill temper; their exasperation was quite real. Hambledon, padding inconspicuously behind in his ancient clothes with a shiny rubber coat over all, found the rain running down the back of his neck until it trickled into the tops of his boots. The streets were almost deserted, which made following particularly difficult, since it was probable that Forgan and Campbell were being watched to see if they were being followed. Hambledon had to drop further and further back and even abandon their route at times to join it again three turnings later.

Finally he saw them turn a corner some distance ahead and hurried after them, only to find, when he rounded the corner himself, that they had entirely disappeared. On one side of the road was the long unbroken fence of the railway-goods yard; on the other were small shops shut for the night and a line of hoardings enclosing wrecked buildings. There was nowhere there that they could be, and Hambledon remembered having heard a car start up and drive away. They must have been picked up by a car, and there was no one to ask which way it had gone.

Hambledon cursed under his breath and turned to walk back towards the Dom. The only possibility of seeing any more of them was to go to the Unter Goldschmied on the chance that they might be taken there, though he admitted to himself that they might equally well be anywhere else within a ten-mile radius of the Cathedral. However, he felt responsible for them since they had come to Germany at his request, so he sighed impatiently and plodded wearily along. To make matters worse, distant thunder began to roll heavily and flashes of lightning lit up the southern sky.

He avoided his usual route by the Hohestrasse; the girls would not think it odd if the old man did not come out on his usual shopping expedition on such a night. He went right down to the river, along the quays, and approached the Unter Goldschmied from the direction of the ruined Rathaus. By this time he was very glad of the increasingly frequent lightning, since, though the light ahead from the one street lamp in the Unter Goldschmied kept him in the right direction, it would be more than easy to take a toss which would break an ankle or even a neck or land one at the bottom of one of those ghastly haunted cellars where a disabled man might lie undiscovered until he died.

At long last he crawled up the side of a hump of rubble from which he could look down on the street lamp only fifty yards away to his right, and to his left on the open space of the Laurenzplatz with the plinth of the missing statue squarely in the middle. Hambledon lay down, parted the tall weeds with his hands, and put his face between them.

There was something going on by the street lamp. The two girls were there in long coats shining with rain and waterproof squares tied over their heads; with them was someone who seemed to be a workman, for he carried a bag of tools and was discussing something with the taller girl. He gestured towards the sky, now alive with lightning, and Magda von Bergen leaned towards him to speak in his ear as the thunder roared overhead. Between the flashes the darkness was intense; the rain stopped suddenly and the cessation made the storm more ominous.

A few minutes later the lights of a car came from the Hohestrasse down Salomonsgasse, which leads to the Laurenzplatz. At once Magda turned with an imperious gesture to the workman, who knelt down at the foot of the lamp pole. Hambledon looked away to watch the car coming slowly and carefully with its headlights turning and dipping as it rolled on the uneven road; a moment later he was aware that the street lamp had gone out. So that was what the workman was there for.

The car crossed the Laurenzplatz till it reached the corner of the Unter Goldschmied and there stopped. Doors opened; five men got out and came along the road towards Hambledon. They were plainly silhouetted against the headlights, walking in two pairs with one ahead. The lightning dazzled the eyes so much that it was hard to see plainly, but there was something very odd about the appearance of one man in each pair.

Just below Hambledon, and not more than twenty yards away, they stopped and there came the sound of voices. Hambledon, who had withdrawn into cover a little, risked another peep and saw that the men who looked so odd were completely hooded. Black hoods covered their heads and faces entirely and had no holes for eyes.

Someone said: "Get on, let's get on," in an impatient voice, and to Hambledon's horror they turned off the road and came directly towards him. He lay completely flat and motionless, hiding his hands and face; the party altered course slightly and passed within five yards of him. He was actually lying close to one of the many tracks which wander about the ruins.

They passed by; footsteps and voices died away. The thunder and lightning had stopped for the moment of their passing; when the storm began again it was perceptibly further off, but, with a rush like a falling torrent, the heavens opened and the rain fell in solid sheets. Hambledon, lying like one dead, could hear a separate little runnel splashing off his shoulders to the ground.

"It only wants that Magda," he said to himself, "to mistake me for a boulder and perch on me, and the evening will just be rounded off nicely." However, he heard no sound of steps or voices, and after what seemed like hours he lifted his head. The car was still standing at the corner of the Laurenzplatz; the lightning showed it dimly, for all its lights were out.

After a time the darkness became slightly less intense, and Hambledon thought it safer to move a few feet further from the path in case the party came back the same way. He accomplished this by a series of caterpillar-like extensions and contractions and eventually terrified himself by rolling suddenly into a crevice, which fortunately was only a couple of feet deep, though at the moment of falling it felt like a bottomless crevasse. He curled himself up at the bottom, pulled the nearest weeds more or less together to cover himself, and waited. The storm died away, the rain eased off and stopped, over his head a few stars came out.

After what seemed the lapse of several lifetimes he heard steps and voices again. Since the night was now quiet he could hear them all round him; it seemed that the meeting had broken up and men were leaving it in all directions. One man came so near that Tommy could hear the weeds brushing against his boots. Over towards the Laurenzplatz a car started up and drove away in low gear.

Hambledon counted a hundred five times slowly after

the last sound had died away, lifted his head cautiously, and sat up. There was no one in sight, and the street lamp in the Unter Goldschmied was once more shining cheerfully from the top of its pole. He rose stiffly to his knees, crawled out of his crevice, and made his way with immense care out of that desolate area. As he slipped in behind Anton's stall to change into his own clothes a pale primrose streak grew and spread across the eastern horizon, and high above his head, upon a broken gable, a thrush began to sing.

## **10** *OLD FATHER TIME*

Forgan and Campbell tramped through the streets on that night of rain and thunder, pausing occasionally under a street lamp to check their route and seeing nothing of Hambledon, whom, indeed, they would not have recognized if they had seen him.

"We're not far from the end of this ceremonial parade," said Forgan, looking at the map once more. "They said we should be met en route, didn't they? Two more turnings and that's the end. Do you suppose they've called off the party on account of the weather?"

"If they have," said Campbell ominously, "and not let us know——"

"We'll leave by the first plane to Paris in the morning."

"Taking the money with us."

"That's the idea," said Forgan. "I rather hope they don't pick us up now; I'd much rather pick up a taxi and go home to bed. What a night. Left here and then left once more. If we haven't seen them by then, they've had it."

They turned left into a long street with the unbroken fence of the railway-goods yard along the opposite side. Thirty yards ahead of them a big limousine car was parked

125

just beyond a street lamppost; as the two men came into the light from the lamp the car door opened and a man stepped out on to the pavement.

"The Herren d'Almeida and Piccione?" he said.

"Who are you?" said Campbell shortly.

"I am sent to convey you to a meeting to discuss oranges."

"Then you might have met us sooner on a night like this," said Campbell, and added in Spanish: "I suppose this is the right fellow, Piccione?"

"It can hardly be anyone else under the circumstances," answered Forgan in the same language.

"Very well," said Campbell, reverting to German, "we will come with you."

He got into the car, followed by Forgan and the German, the door was shut, and the car moved off. There was a second German already in the car and another in front beside the driver.

"Is it far to this place?" asked Campbell, still using a peremptory tone.

"Some distance, mein Herr, yes."

"Be as quick as possible, please," said Campbell. He leaned back in his seat, drew out his cigarette case, and offered Forgan one. At this the two Germans, who were sitting on the small seats facing them, drew down the blinds of the side windows and also of the window between them and the driver. Campbell flashed on his petrol lighter, gave Forgan a light, lit his own cigarette, and then deliberately held it up while he scanned the faces of the Germans opposite. One of them leaned forward and switched on the roof light in the car.

"That is better," said Campbell calmly, and returned his lighter to his pocket.

The car went on and on, turning left and right; the rain beat against the windows and the thunder became louder and nearer; the lightning flashes were visible through the blinds. Forgan and Campbell leaned back in their respective corners and talked intermittently in Spanish about mutual friends, including in a respectful voice a reference to the *caudillo*, Franco. At the end of three quarters of an hour the car turned right and entered upon a road of which the surface was so bad that they were thrown roughly from side to side. Campbell was about to protest, when there were two sharp raps on the glass screen in front.

Immediately the two Germans leaned forward and one said: "We are almost there. I am instructed to beg that the Herren will kindly permit themselves to be blindfolded."

"Certainly not," said Campbell angrily. "Are we, then, enacting an adventure story for schoolboys?"

"An adventure story, perhaps, but not for boys," said the German. He drew what looked like two soft black bags from his pocket and gave one to his companion. "The Herren will not find these uncomfortable; when properly adjusted, there is a slit for the mouth. I must beg the Herren to indulge us in this matter; it is nothing to them, but to us it is our lives."

"Evidently you do not trust us," stormed Campbell, but Forgan intervened.

"Permit the men to have their way, D'Almeida," he said. "They are doubtless but underlings who have received orders, and we do not argue with servants."

"You are right, Piccione, as usual," said Campbell, and they leaned forward to have the hoods put on and adjusted. They were fastened with a band round the neck and were not uncomfortable but completely blinding.

The car stopped; they were helped out and led along a road, then over a rough track where they stumbled and cursed, and finally down a flight of fourteen steps where they were assisted by two men each. There seemed to be more people about at this point. At the bottom of the steps they were led forward upon a level if uneven floor for twenty-five paces; a sharp right turn and another ten paces, then there was a short pause while a door was opened. It was certainly a door, because even through their hoods they could see that there was a tall oblong of light opening before them.

They were led into a room where there was the sound of several people moving about; their hoods were taken off and they blinked in the strong light of an unshaded electric bulb against the low ceiling. It was a large room at least twenty feet square with rough whitewashed walls, a carpet on the floor, a dozen or so chairs standing about, and a long table across the further end with three more chairs behind it. The air was pure and fresh, and there was the quiet hum of an electric motor running, no doubt the air-conditioning plant of whatever building had once stood above this place.

There were only men in the room, nine all told; they had all risen to their feet when Forgan and Campbell were led in. Two of them stood behind the table, and the man who had invited Campbell into the car went round the table and joined them; the other two were a grey-haired man with a beard, the only elderly man in the room, and the Herr Gustav Volkenborn.

"Be seated, gentlemen," said the grey-haired man. "Karl, chairs for our guests. Let me introduce myself, Hans Muller. On my left hand, Franz Pilger, one of your guides, and on my right, Fritz Richter, who had the honour of presenting himself to you at the Excelsior Hotel the other day."

Campbell bowed and presented "my friend and colleague, the Señor Miguel Piccione, and I am Alfonso Demetrio d'Almeida, both entirely at your service."

The preliminaries having been disposed of with, as Campbell remarked afterwards, a series of cracking lies, the meeting got down to business.

"It will, I think, be generally agreed," said Muller, who, whatever his real name was, had undoubtedly been chairman of innumerable meetings before, he had that air, "that the first item on the agenda is for our guests—our very welcome guests—to prove their identity. A formality, of course, but, I fear, a necessary one under the circumstances."

"Oh no, it isn't," said Campbell. "The very first item on the agenda is a complete explanation of why our rooms at the hotel were broken into and our luggage ransacked. The second item——"

"Herr d'Almei——"

"The second item," repeated Campbell, raising his voice, "is an unqualified apology for that outrage!" He leaned back in his chair, folded his arms, and stared coldly at the chairman.

"It would be beyond all measure regrettable," he said

blandly, "to start our first meeting under an easily dispersible cloud of misunderstanding."

"It would indeed," said Campbell grimly. "To all subsequent business regrettably stultifying."

"I am quite sure," said the chairman in a firm voice, "that the distinguished Herren will forgive us when they realize what risks we run in meeting at all, even all friends together, when they consider the odds we have against us, the Occupation Authorities, the police in their pay, the agents of Soviet Russia, and any member of the general public whose interest it is to——"

"If the risks are so great," said Forgan to Campbell, speaking in German, "I begin to wonder whether we ought to proceed with this matter without further consultation with those who sent us."

Campbell nodded thoughtfully. "That is so. But I must point out that we appear to be getting away from item one on the agenda. By whom and why were our suitcases rifled?"

"It was done at my order," said the chairman, "so that we might assure ourselves that you were the right men before we approached you at all."

"Ten thousand horned devils," snarled Campbell, "then why are you pestering us for proofs of identity *now*?"

"Possession of a person's luggage," began the chairman, "is not irrefragable proof of——"

"Are you suggesting we stole it?" roared Campbell.

"Not at all, not at——"

Forgan intervened. "This rather foolish—if I may say so —argument looks like lasting all night," he said in a high clear voice. "I suggest, my dear D'Almeida, that you and I set an example in reasonableness and courtesy. If you will produce your passport and such other evidences of identity as you happen to have with you, I shall be happy to do the same, on condition that these gentlemen present do so also."

Campbell allowed himself to simmer down slightly.

"In deference to your wishes, my dear Piccione, I am prepared to agree. On condition, also, that the apology for which I asked is forthcoming."

"Agree," said Volkenborn to the chairman in a low tone, "agree, or we shall get nowhere."

"But——" said the chairman.

Volkenborn rose to his feet. "I propose to this meeting that a sincere apology be offered to our guests for the clumsy—I admit it—clumsy and discourteous methods which were used towards these gentlemen at their first arrival in Cologne. Let them be assured that nothing was further from our thoughts than to insult them. Our miseries have made us rough; let us realize that and apologize. Will those who agree with this motion say so?"

There was a chorus of "*Ja!*" from those present. Forgan and Campbell looked at each other and nodded.

"We accept that," said Campbell, "and in return, I do not carry my passport about with me—it is in the hotel safe—but here are some of my travellers' cheques"—he threw them down upon the table—"and some letters addressed to me in Madrid and Paris. The letters themselves are, naturally, private," he added pointedly.

Forgan produced a bill from a Madrid tailor for a pair of trousers and a Spanish driving license. The chairman took the papers with a bow and looked at them carefully

one by one, with Volkenborn and the man introduced as
Pilger leaning across on either hand to see them also. When
they had finished the chairman looked up with an air of
surprise.

"These," he said, "are undoubtedly satisfactory so far
as they go, but they are not, of course, the specific papers
which it was arranged for you to bring to this meeting. I
refer to——"

"Careful," murmured Volkenborn.

"You know, of course, to what I refer," said the chairman.

"Of course we do," said Campbell, who had not the faintest idea, because a prolonged search through the Spaniards'
numerous papers had completely failed to unearth anything significant. "Now I will ask you to consider our point
of view. We have been entrusted with something for some
people we were to meet. We do not know them. We received unsigned letters calling us to a mysterious meeting,
and here we are, but how are we to tell that you are indeed those for whom that something was intended? For all
we know, you may be some opposition party or spies of
Soviet Russia or the police; how are we to tell? Forgive me
if I speak frankly. We owe it to those who sent us not to
be fooled in this matter; you will understand that, I am
sure."

"Thank you," said the chairman, and entered into a
whispered conversation with Volkenborn and Pilger. There
was an awkward pause which was broken by a young man at
the back of the room who rose and said that, with respect,
would it not be as well to ask the Spanish gentlemen
bluntly what proofs they would accept? Another asked

if the Herren d'Almeida and Piccione had the papers with them, and Campbell said curtly that they had not. Nor the money, either. They had come to that meeting to be satisfied about bona fides, not to hand out money and secret documents to the first who asked for them.

"We appear to have reached a temporary deadlock," said the chairman as the room filled with a buzz of low-toned argument and the Spanish gentlemen merely sat still and gazed patiently into infinity. At that point there was a movement at the back of the room. Campbell glanced round and saw the door opening, and everybody stood up as an old man came into the room. He was bent in the shoulders and shuffled in his walk; he had untidy grey hair and a beard and wore a shabby frock coat which needed brushing, striped trousers and buttoned boots. His collar was notably low, his tie much resembled a bootlace, and he had an ugly scar upon his neck which looked as though he had at some time tried to cut his throat with a blunt instrument. He peered about him through strong bifocal lenses and carried an umbrella in the last stages of dilapidation; it would not even stay closed without the help of a loop of string which had slipped down and permitted the ribs to flap. The old man was trying to pull up the loop into place as he walked up the room, with the result that some of the company had to dodge the brandished point.

"Look," said Forgan to Campbell in a whisper, "old Father Time."

"Having swopped his scythe for an umbrella," agreed Campbell.

But the old gentleman was received by the company

with a degree of respect amounting to reverence; the young men in the audience stood smartly to attention and the three men behind the table bowed and made place for him with an eager courtesy very curious to watch. He went behind the table, took the chairman's place, glanced about the room for all the world like a lecturer about to address a class, and said in a high piping voice: "Gentlemen, be seated."

The company settled down and the chairman introduced "our visitors, the Herren d'Almeida and Piccione: the Herr Heintz." They bowed with Spanish flourishes; Herr Heintz merely nodded in reply and went on talking to Volkenborn. A moment later he picked up the dreadful umbrella, which he had put down upon the table, rapped sharply with it, and said: "If two young gentlemen at the back will stop talking we will proceed with business. I understand that there is some hitch; what is it?"

The chairman explained.

"I see," said Heintz. "In China, in the latter part of the Ming Dynasty, manners reached such a peak of refinement that the story is told of a host and his guest at the doorway of the dining room who were each so determined not to commit the solecism of preceding the other through the entrance that they both died of starvation upon the doorstep. Let us not emulate them. Gentlemen," addressing Forgan and Campbell, "let me ask you in all friendship, have you no better evidence of identity upon you than a tailor's bill and a couple of letters?"

The visitors smiled politely and examined their wallets in the hope, they said, of finding something more convincing. Forgan uttered a cry of joy, snatched a photograph from among his papers, and handed it up. "That, I believe, will convince you."

Heintz took the print, turned it round, and looked at it with a puzzled expression.

"But this," he said, "is only a portrait of you and your excellent friend in front of our Cathedral."

"What?" said Forgan, completely deflated. "Can I possibly be so foolish—it is the wrong photograph—let me look again, I am sure I have it——"

He took the print back and hunted repeatedly through his wallet and his pockets.

"It is of no use," he said sadly. "Forgotten of God, I have left it behind. I can but beg the distinguished caballero to accept the heartfelt apologies of a——"

Heintz cut him short. "We will take them as read, if you will excuse us. I now suggest that this meeting be adjourned to a date to be arranged. In the meantime, we will consider what proofs we can offer the Herren of identities which we go to considerable pains to conceal. If they agree that such proofs are acceptable, we will produce them at the next meeting, to which the Herren will also bring the matters with which they were entrusted. Agreed? . . . Good. How long did you spend arguing this point before I came? . . . Deplorable, quite deplorable." He picked up his umbrella from the table and began again to push up the circle of string high enough to do some good. "Has anyone else anything further to say? . . . Apparently not. In that case we will wish our kindly visitors *auf Wiedersehen* and thank them for coming. Good night, gentlemen."

## 11 MISSING, TWO SPANIARDS

Campbell and Forgan were hooded once more, led out to the waiting car, and driven away. When eventually the car stopped they were put down in the Hohestrasse, now empty and deserted.

"Any use taking its number?" asked Campbell.

"It won't be, but I have," said Forgan.

"We didn't get much out of that, did we? Some personal descriptions, that's all. I wondered that they let us see them so clearly; I expected a solitary candle, not that electric light. By the way, what was the point of all that funny business with the photograph? It didn't do any good."

"It didn't, did it?" said Forgan meekly.

"All the same, I'd like to see Hambledon while the details are still fresh in my mind."

"Look over your left shoulder and you will," said Hambledon's voice as he moved out from the shadow of Anton's stall.

"Must you pop up like Pepper's ghost?" demanded Forgan. "Sit still, my heart!"

"Sorry," said Tommy. "I only did it to point the moral that it might not have been me standing there. See that archway on the right further on? Wander along and step in there. I'll join you in a moment." He side-stepped through an empty doorway and immediately disappeared.

"We were careless," said Campbell a moment later, "and he was quite right."

"Hush," said Forgan impressively.

They stood in the archway looking about them; there were street lamps still alight in the Hohestrasse, although the darkness was giving way to the grey light of dawn, but they both started nervously when a hand came out of the shadows and drew them further back.

"Do they keep Phospherine in the shops here?" asked Campbell. "I want to buy some."

"Keep your voices down," said Hambledon. "What happened?"

They told him; at the description of the old gentleman with the awful umbrella Hambledon frowned.

"And a scar on his neck? Doesn't suggest anybody to me," he said.

"He was a Big Noise," said Forgan. "They practically fell on their knees when he came in. Right on the spot, too, he settled the whole business in two ups."

"He wasn't so old as he looked," said Campbell. "His hands weren't those of an old man, and his bifocal glasses were a fake. The top part was plain glass; I saw his eyes quite plainly through it, and they weren't an old man's eyes, either. Much too bright. What's more, when he wanted to look at anything close he looked over the bottom half of the lenses. He wasn't shortsighted."

"You've given me an excellent description," said Tommy. "From that I shall be able to make enq——"

"We can do better than that," said Forgan; "we've got

his fingerprints." He took out his wallet and very carefully extracted the photograph he had shown to Heintz.

"I am a fool," said Campbell suddenly.

"No, no," said Forgan earnestly.

"Nice glazed print," said Tommy, taking it carefully by the edges and stowing it away. "I'll take this to Bonn tomorrow and see what they have to say. Tomorrow, I said; later on this morning is what I mean. Nothing else?"

"There must be some papers in our baggage that we haven't found yet," said Forgan.

"Well, you know what to do, don't you?" said Tommy. "If you still can't find them I'll come and have a look, shall I? Well, I'm going to bed for what's left of the night. I'll ring you up when I get back from Bonn."

The headquarters of the Western Allies' Occupation Authority is at Bonn, which is also the seat of the West German Government and a university town as well. The Occupation Authorities do their mysterious business in a large white building with pillars, the flags of the Allies flying from the roof, and smooth lawns in front. Hambledon went straight to the office of the Intelligence Branch and asked for a friend of his who was in charge of it, but Charles Denton was out to lunch. Hambledon handed in the photograph and asked if it were possible to have the prints upon it identified.

"What is this man," he was asked, "what nationality?"

"Almost certainly a German, and probably a high-ranking Nazi."

"We have quite a large selection of records; we'll chase these up for you. Could you—have you anything you want to do in Bonn?"

"I want to give myself some lunch," said Tommy.

"Yes, well, look, come in after lunch and perhaps we'll have something for you, and in any case Denton will be back then."

Hambledon nodded and strolled towards the town. It was a brilliantly fine day, and when he found a very bright new café with small tables on a series of terraces running down to the Cologne road he decided to lunch there. It was an amusing scene; most of the customers were obviously members of the Allied Commission with their wives and families, but there were also German government officials, students from Bonn University, and a sprinkling of such elderly professors of marked individuality as one finds in any ancient university city. There seems to be something about the scholastic life which develops idiosyncrasy and a contempt for public opinion.

Tommy ate an extremely good lunch and followed it up with a cup of coffee, a liqueur brandy, and a cigar. There came along the road from the Allied Commission's offices a young man on a bicycle, looking eagerly about him; he saw Hambledon on the terrace, sprang from his cycle, ran up the steps, and spoke to him.

"Excuse me, sir, Major Denton sent me. Could you please come back to the office at once, as he wants to see you urgently?"

Hambledon reached the office to find Denton striding about his room in what was, for him, a state of some excitement.

"Hullo, Hambledon! I say, those fingerprints on that photo of yours——"

"Well?"

"Where the hell did you get them? They look quite fresh."

"They are fresh. They were made last night——"

"Where?"

"In Cologne. Whose are they?"

"We're not quite sure yet. Did you see the man who made them?"

"No, but I've got a description of him." Hambledon began to repeat Campbell's description of the grey-whiskered old gentleman with the sham bifocal glasses and the ugly scar on his neck, the curiously bright eyes and smooth muscular hands. When he went on to describe the dusty black coat and striped trousers, the low collar and the insubordinate umbrella, it dawned upon him suddenly that he was describing someone he had himself seen, and his voice trailed off. Seen quite recently—where?

"Go on, what's the matter?"

"He's here, that's what. Sitting in that café where I had lunch; he was still there when I——"

"Come on," said Denton, and left the building with long strides. They reached the café; the lunch hour was over and most of the small tables were empty, but near the end of the middle terrace there still sat an elderly shabby figure. Hambledon ran up the steps with Denton at his elbow and said: "There you are."

"Is that the man?" said Denton incredulously, and pointed at him with outstretched arm. The old man looked up and instantly his own arm shot out; there was a sharp crack and a thud close to Hambledon as Denton reeled against him and slid to the ground. Hambledon, stooping, tried to catch him and thereby probably saved his own life, for there was a second crack and a bullet sailed over his head. Women screamed, mothers snatched up their children, wise men dived under tables, and waiters rushed out of the café, but the elderly professor sprang to his feet, ran lightly across the lower terrace, put one hand on the low wall which divided it from the road, and neatly vaulted over.

A small black saloon car had been parked in the road for some time with a young man reading a book in the driver's seat. At the first shot he dropped the book, started the engine, and drove slowly forward to meet the professor at the point where he leaped the wall. The old gentleman tore open the car door and scrambled inside as the car accelerated and shot out of sight in the direction of Cologne.

Denton was on his feet again in time to see the professor go; leaning on Hambledon's shoulder, he said: "Blast! The one that got away."

"Cheer up," said Tommy. "Spry for his age, isn't he? Are you much hurt?"

"No. Only gone through the top of my shoulder. I fell down from pure surprise, I think."

Policemen arrived on the terrace and kept back the crowd which had begun to gather. Tommy said: "He's left his umbrella, look. We'll have that. You sit down." He went across to the table where the fugitive had been sitting and picked up the umbrella; as he did so a Luger automatic slid out of it and fell to the ground.

"So that's where he carried it," said Tommy, returning with his trophies. "You're for hospital, my lad, and what Liese will say to me about this I dread to think."

"I'll ring her from the hospital," said Denton, being helped down the steps to a taxi. "She's here in Bonn."

"Then I'm going back to Cologne," said Hambledon.

The car was sought with diligence but in vain. It was not in any way remarkable and nobody had noticed it or its number; there was even a difference of opinion about its make. One Englishman who had to leap for his life when the car started remembered the driver and described him: a fair-haired young man in the early twenties with a broad face, a straight nose, a round chin, and hard blue eyes a little too near together. "He didn't care if he did run me down, I could see that," said the Englishman angrily. "Young hooligan! Typical Hitler Youth."

"Dear me," said Hambledon thoughtfully.

He spent the rest of the day telling his story in detail to the Intelligence Office, after which he returned to Cologne by express tram and immediately rang up the Dom Hotel to speak to Forgan and Campbell, but they were not there; he rang up later in the evening, but they still had not returned. When he telephoned again in the morning and received the same reply he became uneasy. There was no reason why the two men should not have gone somewhere else for the night; they were free agents and they might quite well have gone to Frankfurt or Wiesbaden for a change, but it was a little odd that they had not told him they were going. The hotel people said that the gentlemen had not spoken of going away.

He rang up again after lunch. The Spanish gentlemen had not come back, but they were not likely to be away long, all their luggage was still in their rooms.

Hambledon put down the receiver and went out to find Spelmann.

"I want to engage you officially upon this search for my missing friends," said Hambledon. "I want you to start at once, abandoning all else."

"I will do so with pleasure," said Spelmann, "all the more so as my enquiry into the Torgius case seems to have dried up for the moment. I have, as it were, some lines out and I am waiting for the fish to bite."

"I make no promises," said Hambledon, "but it is just possible that if you find out what has happened to my friends and who is responsible, you may discover at the same time why two men were hanged from a girder in the Unter Goldschmied."

Spelmann looked hard at him. "May I say this to the Herr? I begin to think that you—you have an English phrase, what is it?—you detach my leg, is it not? You are not entirely the simple English tourist with the tweed trousers, *hein*?"

"Never mind my trousers for the moment. I'll tell you this much, that if you unravel this mystery you really will be a famous detective, though I doubt if you'll get your photograph in the newspapers over it. Now, I particularly don't want to go to the Dom Hotel myself to ask about my friends D'Almeida—he's the tall one with red hair—and Piccione, because it is very undesirable indeed that anyone should know that we are friends. I have never been there to see them, and we have been very careful where we met. You can think up some story. Now go to it."

Forgan and Campbell came down to breakfast as usual on the morning after the meeting and strolled out into the square. They felt rather at a loose end; Hambledon had gone to Bonn for the day, the Silver Ghosts were not likely to get into touch with them again at once, and they were a little tired of wandering about the ruins of Cologne. When, therefore, they were approached outside the door of the hotel by a tout desiring to enlist them in a motor tour of the Siebengebirge—the Seven Mountains—they looked at each other.

"Bonn," urged the tout, "Bonn, the university city, the seat of government—all their seats, German and Allied—Königswinter, the Drachenfels where Siegfried killed the dragon and his blood makes the only red wine in all the Rhine Valley; lovely scenery, gentlemen, nice inns, good food—only five marks——"

"Well?" said Campbell.

"Let's go," said Forgan, and they bought their tickets from the man then and there.

"We call for you at the door of your hotel here," said the man. "No walking out to find the vehicle parked somewhere else, no which-one-is-it, no bother."

"Splendid," said Campbell. When they went in to lunch they told the reception clerk that they were going on an autobus tour that afternoon starting at one o'clock; they would be in the lounge at that time and would like to be called when the bus stopped at the door.

"I was a little surprised," said the hotel clerk to Spelmann. "These buses do not as a rule go round to the hotels to pick up their passengers, but there are many tours and this might be a new one; besides, what business was it of mine? The Herren had made their own arrangements; the bus came to the door, I sent the chass' to tell

them so, they got in and drove away. That is all I know.
. . . No, I did not see the bus outside the door, not to say
really see it. I look through the doorway and see a tall
narrow strip of green vehicle with seats inside and a white
roof and I say to myself, 'That is a bus.' I do not go outside
to examine it; I see buses every day. . . . No, I did not actually see the gentlemen get in, I saw them pass along inside to their seats. The bus then drove away; they generally
do, in my experience. . . . No, I told you I did not go
out to look at it. *Gott verdammt nochmal,* how should I
know what the direction board had on it? Go and ask some
of the idlers who hang about the square all day with nothing to do."

Spelmann did, but nobody seemed to have noticed this
autobus. A tour to the Siebengebirge starting at thirteen
hours? They had never seen one. The Columbus Tours had
a bus on that route that day, but it did not start until
fourteen hours, probably he had got the time wrong.

He went back to the hotel and verified that this particular bus really did start at one o'clock and not at two and
that in any case Columbus Tours started from St. An-
dreas Church and did not drive round the hotels. He went
out again into the square to look for inspiration; over
against the Cathedral the official photographer was posing
a group of three small children with their parents standing
proudly behind their accomplishments. Spelmann waited
until the transaction was finished and then went across to
the photographer.

"Were you by any chance taking photos here at thirteen hours on the day before yesterday?"

"I was, yes. Did I, then, photograph some dangerous criminal?"

"They all look like that when you've done with them. Would you mind if I looked at the films you took about then?"

Visitors sometimes like to be taken standing in front of their hotel. "That? Oh yes, that's where we were staying. Not a bad pub, actually," they say airily when it's the Crillon in Paris or its equivalent elsewhere. The bus must have stood outside the Dom Hotel for some minutes while Forgan and Campbell were detached from their after-lunch liqueurs in the lounge, and there was just a chance that the camera had recorded it. Spelmann looked carefully through Monday's films in the photographer's little workshop.

"I can't tell you," he said, handing Spelmann a magnifying glass, "at exactly what time any of these were taken. I know the earlier ones and the later ones, but when it comes to exact times such as are required to establish an alibi——"

"That's all right," said Spelmann absently.

"If you'd like a print taken off any one of those you've only to say so. It won't take five minutes."

"Thank you," said Spelmann suddenly. "May I have one of this one?"

He got his print hastily dried off in little over five minutes. "It will not last," said the photographer, "it will fade, it will come up in blotches, for it is insufficiently washed. If you would like a better one——"

"This will do beautifully, thank you," said Spelmann,

patting him on the shoulder. "You are a good comrade, indeed you are."

"I suppose I may not ask—it would be indiscreet of me to enquire——"

"Horribly indiscreet. Never mind, perhaps it will all come out one day."

Spelmann went to Hambledon with his prize. "The mysterious autobus," he said, "here it is in a photograph, is it not? It is true that you only see the tail of it behind that car, but we have the number, mein Herr; also, you can see a little of the direction board, there, '—stal, Eberjagen.' Eberjagen is in the Siebengebirge. The Herr knows that district?"

"I used to," said Hambledon. "You'd better hire a car."

As soon as Spelmann had started in pursuit of the route followed by Autobus Number BR 87208 with Forgan and Campbell on board, Hambledon went to the Dom Hotel. Since his friends were no longer in residence, there was no reason why he should avoid the place. Besides, there were those papers, whatever they were, hidden somewhere in their luggage; the modelmakers had failed to find them, but Tommy had more confidence in his own talent for discovering hiding places than he had in theirs. For one thing, he had had a great deal more practice. A quiet hour alone in their room might be most rewarding. He knew the number.

He had also known the hotel very well during the First World War, for he had lived there. It was true that that was more than thirty years earlier, but the place had not been rebuilt in the meantime, rather *au contraire*, as the

Frenchman said when asked if he had lunched on the cross-Channel steamer. There was a good deal less of the Dom Hotel than there was before Hitler's war, but what remained was substantially unaltered. He went into the lounge and ordered a drink, waited until the reception clerk was absent from his desk for a moment, and quietly walked upstairs.

Forgan and Campbell shared a double room on the second floor; Hambledon, having seen their key, knew what type of lock it was and had come equipped to unlock the door. It was only to choose a moment when there was nobody about in the short passage. He stood back to allow a man, his wife, and a curly-headed child to pass him and then walked straight to the door, his footsteps inaudible upon the passage carpet. He was just about to start operations when he heard a sound inside; someone had dropped a small object which bounced and rolled. There was some one in there already, either the chambermaid, in which case he had, of course, "come into the wrong room. So sorry," or someone who had no business there.

He turned the door handle quietly and carefully. The door was not locked; he opened it. In the mirror opposite he saw a man close to him, by the chest of drawers behind the door, and he had papers in both hands, as though he were sorting through them.

Tommy hit him behind the ear with all the force he could muster and the automatic already in his hand. The man, who had in that instant dropped the papers and dived into his pocket for his gun, fell face downwards upon the carpet with his revolver beside him. Hambledon turned him over and recognized him from one of certain photo-

graphs and descriptions he had been shown at Bonn; he was
an escaped criminal, wanted by the police.

Tommy shut the room door and looked about him. On
the top of the chest of drawers was the toilet case which
Campbell had, as it were, inherited from D'Almeida, a
soft leather case about eight inches by twelve with a zip
fastener running round three sides of it. Its contents, hairbrushes, razor, soapbox, clothesbrush, and so forth, were
turned out upon the chest of drawers and the watered-silk
lining of the case itself had been slit from corner to corner
diagonally.

"So that's where the papers were," said Tommy. "Very
neat, but I think that in your place, Forgan, I should have
seen that."

He gathered up all the fallen papers and put them away
in his inside coat pocket, repacked the toilet case and
fastened it, listened at the door to make sure the coast was
clear, and walked unhurriedly out of the room, shutting
the door behind him. Once out of the hotel, he went to
the railway station and rang up the police from there.

"I believe you are looking for an escaped criminal named
Mulder from Düsseldorf?" he said. "You are, yes. He is in"
—he gave Forgan's room number—"on the second floor of
the Dom Hotel. He is unconscious at the moment and I
should think he'll sleep on for another half-hour, but it
might be as well to collect him as soon as possible because
he is armed."

"Thank you," said the official voice at the other end.
"What is your name, please?"

But the only answer was a click as Hambledon hung
up the receiver. He went across the square again to the

Muserkeller, stood himself a glass of beer, and awaited events. Almost at once a "Peter-car"—P for Peter and also for Police—whirled up to the hotel door, and a sergeant and two constables alighted and went in. Ten minutes later one of the constables reappeared and spoke to the driver, who nodded and took the Peter-car round towards the hotel's back door. Another ten minutes and the police car came again across the square, driving more slowly this time. It seemed very full of men. . . .

Hambledon went back to the Gürzenich Hotel, locked himself in his bedroom, and looked interestedly through the rescued papers. There was an official letter from the Spanish organization addressed to "the most excellent Señor Gustav Volkenborn" testifying to the extreme reliability under the most adverse circumstances of "the most illustrious Señores" d'Almeida and Piccione, the bearers of the letter, which ended formally: "May God preserve your worship many years."

"Not if I have any say in the matter," said Tommy.

The next paper he opened was a short list of the business with which they were authorized to deal. The money, twenty thousand German marks, to be handed over. Arrangements to be made for simplifying future communications. Arrangements to be made for the transfer of bonds held by Spanish banks to banks in Switzerland, the application forms sent herewith to be signed by the applicant in person.

"This bunch of stuff is the application forms, I suppose," said Tommy, and unfolded them rather casually. The next moment he sat down heavily upon his bed, which bounced him, and said: "Oh, Christopher! Oh, Columbus!"

There were more than a dozen of these forms, each dealing with sums of money running into thousands of pounds sterling, and each, after the formal printed headings, began in typescript: "I, Martin Bormann . . ."

Hambledon got up and washed his face violently in cold water; this process is said to quicken the faculties. Then he sat down on his bed and looked at his treasures once more; the name was still there, though he had half expected it to have disappeared. "I, Martin Bormann," with an address in the province of Sevilla. The office which issued these forms was in Cádiz.

"Dear me," said Tommy aloud. "So he is alive and living near Cádiz, as was said by the voice of rumour normally a liar but now a sub-office of Reuters, Press Association, Exchange Telegraph, and Central News and so justified of her children like Jerusalem, though what should take my mind from Bormann to Jerusalem unless it's the attraction of opposites I really don't know. I think I'm a little excited. So those meetings in the Unter Goldschmied's shelly smellers—smelly cellars—are the Silver Ghosts and Bormann is behind them. I wonder who the alleged professor was who pipped Denton, and whether the said pillar of learning has rolled up again in Bonn. I shouldn't think so, though nobody notices professors in their own places. To be accurate, they do notice them but don't believe it. If I want to disguise myself I shall wreathe myself in seaweed, carry a large glass jar full of tiddlers, and call myself a professor of meteorology. Denton must see this, so I to Bonn."

He put the papers well down in an inside pocket of his jacket and fastened up the mouth of the pocket with safety pins. On the way downstairs he remembered Spelmann in a hired car trailing a counterfeit autobus tour round the Seven Mountains; there was no knowing what time he would be back. He told the hotel clerk that he was going to see some friends at Bonn and departed in haste for the tram.

Denton was still at his office when Hambledon was shown in, saying: "I've got something to show you, by heck I have. Look here," and dragging safety pins away from his pocket.

"Hambledon, I've been trying to get you on the telephone; those fingerprints you brought us——"

"This is far more thrilling," interrupted Hambledon, pulling the papers out of their envelope. "Look at that, it's Martin Bormann, his own self, transferring——"

"So are the fingerprints," drawled Denton.

"What?"

"The fingerprints. On the photograph. Of the man who shot at me—— By the way, there were some more on the umbrella, so it is the same man."

Hambledon abandoned his papers for the moment.

"Who is the same man as what?"

"You aren't listening," said Denton severely. "The man at the meeting in Cologne is the same man who popped at me in the café——"

"Heaven save us," said Hambledon, "we knew that."

"And his prints," said Denton deliberately, "are those of Martin Bormann."

"What? Do you mean that grizzle-wigged old gink in the gig-lamps—— But of course he wasn't old."

"No. He's a man in the early fifties at most. When we

looked up his fingerprints here we thought they were Bormann's, but those we have are very bad specimens and we
aren't all that expert. So we sent them over to Scotland
Yard for confirmation, and they did. So they are."

"Bless my soul," said Hambledon blankly. "Tell me, what
do you know about Bormann? I don't believe I'd ever heard
of him—or nothing important—till Hitler named him in his
will as the next Führer."

"He's a damned clever man," said Denton. "He kept himself right in the background all the time; he never appeared
in group photographs nor even in any of the cine films,
amateur or professional, of Life and Laughter with Adolf.
I can't think how he managed to avoid them, for goodness
knows there were miles of 'em. There's one of him reading
the marriage contract at the wedding of Eva's sister and
Jockey-General Fegelein, but even that's a bad one. He
never figured in pep talks or sparkling anecdotes in the press,
but the more we find out about him, Hambledon, the more
obvious it becomes that he was the power behind the
throne. The groggier Hitler became, the more Bormann in-
creased, till towards the end when Göring was discredited
and Goebbels a mass of hysteria, Hitler was the merest fig-
urehead and Bormann was Das Reich—only nobody knew
it. Even in the funeral bunker he only sat in a corner writing by the hour, and nobody took much notice of him.
Hanna Reitsch, the airwoman, you remember, told us that,
and she was there."

"Queer," said Hambledon. "What does he look like by
nature?"

"Dark curly hair retreating from the temples, high forehead, nose straight and almost in a line with the forehead,

arched eyebrows, neat features. Not very tall, five foot six
or seven, but looked taller because he is of slight build and
has long legs for his height. Long slim hands. I said he is of
slight build and so he is, but he has unexpectedly wide
shoulders without being deep-chested."

"I see. Like a king on a playing card. Very convenient,
that; you face your adversary looking like King Kong, then
you turn sideways and vanish. What uniform did he wear?"

"Didn't wear one."

"Odder and odder. But those masses of grey whiskers and
long hair, Denton, they can't be all false, surely."

"Perhaps they're his own," said Denton. "You can grow
a lot of hair in five years."

"Grey hair?"

"He could have dyed it or bleached it, whatever the
process is called. Look at women."

"What for?"

"As an example of what can be done with hair. Not for
any other purpose at the moment."

"Oh, very well," said Hambledon. "Now you can look at
my finds. These were concealed in D'Almeida's luggage."

Denton looked them through and said there was enough
there to keep the Allied Commission broody for weeks,
"and if your friends Forgan and Campbell want them I'm
afraid they'll be unlucky."

"They've disappeared, Denton," said Hambledon, and
told him the story.

"Too bad," said Denton. "Cheer up, they may yet return.
People do."

"I must go," said Hambledon. "I've got to see Spelmann
in Cologne tonight; he may have some news for me."

He returned to Cologne and went straight to Spelmann's office. There was a light in the first-floor window; Hambledon opened the street door and went upstairs.

Spelmann reported that he had tracked out the route of Autobus Number BR 87208 without much difficulty. It had followed exactly the route of the Columbus Tours bus an hour later, stopping at the same places: Bonn, Beuel, Königswinter, Bad Honnef, Schmelztal, and Eberjagen. It had stopped for some time at Eberjagen to allow the passengers to stretch their legs and obtain refreshments; so did the Columbus Tours bus in its turn. Nothing out of the ordinary had been seen at any of these places and if, as was probable, it had returned to Cologne by the Autobahn there was no reason why anyone should have noticed it. The only odd thing he had been able to discover was that this autobus had apparently run upon that day only, since no one had seen it before or since.

"There is also," said Spelmann, "the curious incident of the other two Spanish gentlemen at the Dom Hotel. I do not suppose that it has any bearing on—— The Herr appears surprised?"

"Tell me about them," urged Tommy. "Who are they and what happened?"

"Their names are Bonamour and Cierra. The Herr knows them?"

"By name only," said Hambledon, remembering that these were the names under which the genuine D'Almeida and Piccione had been arrested in Paris. "I did not expect them to come here, that's all. I thought they were somewhere in the middle of the South Atlantic Ocean."

"Drowned, the Herr means?"

156

"Heaven forbid! On a ship. They must have—er—changed their minds. What were you going to tell me?"

"Only that they arrived at the Dom Hotel about midday yesterday. They booked rooms, sent up their luggage, and then asked the reception clerk if he could change American dollars. He said he could not, so they went out of the hotel. The Herr knows that there is a currency black market here as elsewhere; there are men who hang about the doors of hotels and ask foreign visitors if they want to sell dollars or Belgian francs or what have you. The Spanish gentlemen were spoken to by a couple of men just outside the door, and after a few minutes' conversation they all walked away together. Mein Herr, these Spanish visitors also have not returned."

Hambledon stared, began to laugh, stopped suddenly, and looked thoughtful. There was no doubt that the entry of the real D'Almeida and Piccione into international politics had been singularly unhappy, but it might quite easily be a great deal worse than that. The Silver Ghosts were a mistrustful and violent company at the best of times; what they would do to duplicate Spanish emissaries hardly bore thinking about. Besides, it doubled the danger to Forgan and Campbell.

"This was—when did you say?"

"Yesterday midday. Twenty-four—thirty hours ago."

"Oh. Oh dear. Perhaps they have merely gone off on the ran-tan and will turn up again with severe headaches."

"It is to be hoped so," said Spelmann doubtfully, "but they acted unusually promptly, did they not? Visitors usually have lunch first."

"Oh, do they? Yes, I suppose they do, now you mention it. I was——"

"One other thing I did," said Spelmann. "I went to the motor license office at Bonn as we passed through this morning; I have a friend who works there. The car number BR 87208 is not an autobus at all; it is a *Volkswagen* belonging to a plumber at Neuss."

Every trace of amusement was wiped off Tommy's face and he sat perfectly still for a moment. "Faked number plates," he said slowly. "Why did you keep that bit of news to the last?"

"To speak truth, I did not wish to tell the Herr," said Spelmann gently. "I myself do not like that piece of news."

"Give me the photograph again."

Spelmann passed it across the table together with a pocket magnifying glass he always carried. "The numbers are quite clear," he said sadly. "It is not as though someone had merely remembered it or perhaps written it down wrong, and at Bonn my friend allowed me to see the entry with my own eyes."

Hambledon gave him back the print and the magnifying glass and again sat quite still, looking at the floor. Forgan and Campbell were, as he knew quite well from past experience, sudden and unaccountable men who might at any moment depart without warning in pursuit of some ingenious idea. He had been genuinely anxious at their disappearance, but he realized at this point how much he had been subconsciously relying on its being a voluntary disappearance. "Another of their devilments" had been at the back of his mind and he had really been expecting them to turn up at any moment with an air of innocence and a long story, told in duet, about some horribly efficient outrage like the disposal of D'Almeida and Piccione in Paris. Hambledon's own imagination was fertile enough, but not by the most elastic stretching could it be made to cover their departure in a bus with faked number plates of their own arranging. They had been decoyed away because they were under suspicion, and this, of all moments, was the one which the real D'Almeida and Piccione had chosen to arrive in Cologne. Now they also had disappeared.

Forgan and Campbell could talk themselves out of most entanglements, but they had been away now for more than two days. It is of no use to talk to those who will not listen. . . .

Hambledon looked up at last, and Spelmann drew back in his chair at the sight of that normally pleasant face so grim and hard.

"Tell me," said Hambledon, "suppose you wanted to hire an autobus for a day or so, to drive it yourself, could you do so? Where would you get it from?"

"Certainly, mein Herr. The autobus people would prefer to send their own driver, no doubt, but if one gave some plausible excuse, paid a big enough deposit, and satisfied them that your driver could drive, they would let the bus out on those terms. I have known it to be done for club outings and so forth, to save expense. As for where they would get it from, I should say that in this case the answer is anywhere except in Cologne. Bonn, Aachen, Düren, Düsseldorf, Solingen——"

Hambledon made a little gesture with his hands.

"I can try every possible place in Cologne," continued Spelmann. "It is a little late tonight, but they may not all be shut, and tomorrow——"

"Do so," said Hambledon curtly.

"At once," said Spelmann, and went.

Hambledon sat still a few minutes longer and then got up suddenly and went down to Anton's stall to change into his workman's clothes. Magda von Bergen and the blond Sophie were by this time so used to seeing him plodding along the Unter Goldschmied and back that they took no notice of him except to call him *"alt Liebchen"* occasionally, and once Sophie gave him a cigarette. He could walk right up to them without alarming them; if they were on duty tonight something might be done if he had to strangle both of them in the process. He walked up the Hohestrasse, round by the Gürzenich, and down the Unter Goldschmied, but there was no sign of either of them. Not one of their nights, evidently. He went back to Anton's and changed again into his ordinary clothes. Back to his hotel in case there was a telephone message from Spelmann. There was none. He went out again, driven by unbearable restlessness, and his feet carried him to Spelmann's office.

At his knock Spelmann opened the door a crack and looked out, opened it wide, and said: "Thank God it is you. I have this moment been telephoning your hotel. Come in."

On one of Spelmann's four chairs sat the blond girl from the Unter Goldschmied, with her face disfigured with crying and her smooth fair hair all in disorder. It looked as though she had been tearing at it. When Hambledon went in she sprang to her feet with a wild look of absolute terror.

"Calm yourself," said Spelmann in a soothing voice, "calm yourself, Fräulein. This is a kind man who will not hurt you. Mein Herr, the Fräulein Sophie Maeder."

Hambledon bowed.

"Fräulein Maeder has come here for protection," said

Spelmann. "She has run away from the Unter Goldschmied because terrible things have been happening. Tell the Herr, *liebes* Fräulein, for he is English and very powerful."

She sat down with a bump, as though her legs had given way, and said: "Lock the door."

"Certainly," said Spelmann, doing so. "Now then. Fräulein Maeder says that the organization have taken the Fräulein Magda von Bergen and the Englishman, Herr Yeoman. She dodged away in the dark and escaped. Now begin at the beginning, my dear, and tell this gentleman all you have told me as far as we got, and then finish the story."

Sophie wiped her eyes, blew her nose, sat upright, and began.

"The Herr George Yeoman was in love with Magda when he first came here and she with him—I think. He was sent away and then went home, but he used to write and at first she answered. Then the young men came back from the war; she knew them all, friends of her brothers in the old days. After a while they started a sort of club and it turned into this—I mustn't say their name, I daren't——"

"The Silver Ghosts, Fräulein," said Hambledon gravely. "Please go on."

"You know that name?" she whispered. "You mustn't say it; men have been hanged for saying it, hanged from a hook in the ceiling——" She shuddered so violently that her teeth chattered.

"Spelmann," said Hambledon, "have you a small glass in this room? To drink from."

"I have," said Spelmann, opening a cupboard, "but nothing to put in it."

"I have," said Tommy, producing a flask he had dropped

into his pocket with some idea that if he found Forgan
and Campbell they might be glad of the contents. "Drink
a little of this, Fräulein; it is cognac, it won't hurt you."

She sipped it, sipped again, and left off shivering so violently.

"Go on with your story."

"Magda's Englishman came tonight to the Unter Goldschmied and said he'd been over at Köln-Deutz thinking.
He said he didn't know what she was doing, but it was
something bad and it had got to stop. She was to go back
to her room and pack up and go to England with him and
get married. She laughed at him and he said it wasn't a
joke. She said he was to go away and never come back, and
he said not without her. Then she lost her temper, but he
only stood there and waited, then she cried and he put his
arms round her and kissed her."

"One moment," said Hambledon. "Where did all this
take place? In the Unter Goldschmied, tonight?"

"It started there, then when he wouldn't go away we went
back among the heaps where nobody could see us. Why?"

"Never mind. Go on."

"I kept trying to go away, but she wouldn't let me. When
he kissed her she clung round his neck and begged him to
go. She said if they caught him they would hang him as
they did young Franz Kahn, with a rope from a hook in the
ceiling, with his hands bandaged together not to show
marks of being tied——"

Spelmann moved suddenly, but Hambledon looked at
him once and he did not speak.

"—all because he made a joke at a party about Silver
Ghosts walking when he was drunk. Then when he'd left

off wriggling they took him down, unbandaged his hands, and hung him again on that girder where they found him in the morning."

"Did you see all this, Sophie?" asked Hambledon.

"No, no, nor the other one, nor did Magda, but one of the boys told her about it."

"The other being Karl Torgius," said Hambledon.

"Do you know everything?" she whispered.

"Not everything. Go on."

"She told him all this to make him go away, and I heard it too—I couldn't help it—I didn't know it before. Then all in an instant they jumped at us out of the dark and got Magda and her Englishman, but I ran away; I'd got this dark dress on, they didn't see me, and I expect they're dead by now and they'll kill me, too, because I heard all about the hangings—— I don't want to die," she said, sobbing. "Get me away, please get me away——"

"What time," said Hambledon to Spelmann, "is the last express tram to Bonn?"

Spelmann looked at his watch. "In thirty-five minutes from now."

"Good. May I use your phone?"

Hambledon had to wait a few minutes for his call to go through, and Sophie began talking very fast.

"I must go a long long way away where nobody's ever heard of me. Karl Torgius wouldn't go to the meeting; he knew they were after him, so he stayed in his own house and they came and hung him in his own garage and took the body to the Unter Goldschmied on a barrow covered over with bananas. Bananas. I was there with Magda that night and I saw them come with the barrow. I wondered why bananas, but we weren't allowed to ask questions; we were sent to keep watch down the road and then home and in the morning when we——"

Hambledon held up his hand for silence, and Sophie stopped as though switched off.

"Is that——" He mentioned a number and asked for an extension number. "Who's that speaking? Hambledon here. . . . The last express tram—yes, tram—to Bonn from Cologne, please meet it without fail and collect from it the Fräulein Sophie Maeder, age about twenty-three, fair hair, blue eyes, height five foot four or thereabouts, dressed in dark blue, no stockings, blue shoes, carries a brown handbag. She has been a great help to us and is in considerable danger; take great care of her. She must be protected and got away somewhere, preferably out of the country. I'm coming over in the morning and we'll see about it then. By the way, you'd better have something she can recognize you by; carry a roll of pink blotting paper. Urgent, don't fall down on this. . . . Good. . . . Splendid. Good night, see you tomorrow."

He replaced the receiver and turned to Sophie. "Now you pull yourself together like a good girl. You haven't finished the brandy; drink it up. I am going to take you to catch the Bonn tram. You heard what I said on the telephone, didn't you? You will be met at the other end by an Englishman, a short fair young man in a grey suit carrying a roll of pink blotting paper in his left hand. He'll look after you, you can go with him without fear, and I'll come and see you in the morning. I think we'd better start, it's some distance from here. I'm not walking with you. I shall be just behind; I can watch you better that way. See this gun?" said

Tommy, producing his automatic. "I shall have that in my hand all the time, and if anyone attempts to stop you I shall shoot him dead. By the way, have you got the money for the fare? Don't worry about hotel bills, you'll be with friends. Well, now, shall we go?"

## *13*  PETER–CAR

Hambledon saw Sophie Maeder safely away on the tram
and returned to Spelmann. "She'll be all right. She's got
plenty of pluck, really; she marched on like a little soldier
with me slinking behind. Now listen to me. I am going to
Bonn tomorrow to consult the authorities about this business, but if Magda von Bergen and George Yeoman are not
at home again before I start, it means putting the police on
it. It's getting too much for us two men to deal with. There
are my two friends, there are the other two Spaniards, that's
four; with Magda and Yeoman that's six. I remember——"
He stopped abruptly.

"Remember what?"

"—my chambermaid telling me she'd seen a man hanging
and I told her it would have been much worse if there had
been a row of them. Well, perhaps it won't happen. If the
police are called in, Spelmann, it will be done from Bonn
and by picked men. Plain-clothes police mainly, I expect.
I think that's all for tonight. Will you go over to this address at Köln-Deutz early tomorrow and ask if Herr Yeoman
has returned and come to me at my hotel before nine? I'll
go to Magda's flat and see if she's there and then get off to
Bonn."

166

Tommy Hambledon went back to his hotel and was talking to the night porter over a final nightcap when the telephone rang, a call for him from Bonn. He had to be careful what he said, as the telephone stood openly in the office with no nonsense about a soundproof call box.

"Yes," he said, "speaking. . . . What? . . . What? . . . You must have missed her; I told you—— Oh, I see. . . . Yes. . . . No, I see. . . . It doesn't look as though you could have missed her. . . . No, quite. There doesn't seem to be anything else you can do tonight. . . . Yes, possible, I suppose, but I doubt it. . . . All right. I'll see you in the morning about ten. Good-bye."

The young man with the roll of pink blotting-paper had rung up to say that no one remotely resembling Sophie Maeder was on the tram which he had been told to meet.

Since there was no news in the morning of Magda von Bergen or George Yeoman, Hambledon went, in a state of fury and exasperation, to Bonn. He had promised the girl she should be safe and she had been snatched away from him; she had given him a good deal of information, but there was a great deal more he wanted to ask her when she was calmer; now it seemed probable that she would be silent forever and his questions remain unasked. When he remembered that it was only his pity for her condition which had prevented him from questioning her all night, and that if he had been less softhearted she would certainly have been with him still, he felt quite sick. Enquiries could and should be made, but he was convinced that they would be useless.

The chief of the Cologne police received a telephone call which took him also to Bonn for a conference; he returned to Cologne in the afternoon and had several interviews in

his private office, after which many orders were issued.
There came from Bonn in the same afternoon some half
dozen men in ordinary civilian dress who yet walked and
looked about them with a certain air of authority. They
were met at the station by the deputy chief of the Cologne
police, who took them by circuitous routes to the area between the Hohestrasse and the ruined Rathaus.

"This is the district referred to in your instructions," he
said.

Later that evening Spelmann was walking down the
Hohestrasse, glancing quickly about him as usual, when he
saw coming towards him a young man named Fitzner who
had been another of Volkenborn's bright young friends before the war. Fitzner was walking slowly with his head bent;
when he was about twenty yards from Spelmann he looked
up suddenly and their eyes met. Fitzner started, hesitated
for a moment, and turned off through a gap in the ruins so
as to avoid meeting the detective.

This was too much for Spelmann, who did not lack personal courage. He came to the Salomonsgasse and turned
down it, looking to his left across the rubble heaps for Fitzner. A few minutes later he saw Fitzner's head peer round
a corner and immediately disappear; Spelmann went after
him.

"There is something going on here," he said. "This young
man is up to some mischief."

The pursuit continued along the little scrambling paths
among the ruins, crossed the Unter Goldschmied not far
from the street lamp, and led on into the wilds again. Spelmann would lose Fitzner for minutes together and then
see him again across a clear space. Once he got near enough

to him to call his name, but Fitzner merely broke into a run.

The call was also heard by six authoritative men in plain clothes who had come from Bonn that day to look into things in the Unter Goldschmied area. They were walking about in order to obtain, by daylight, a general idea of the lie of the land which they expected to patrol in darkness. At that moment they were grouped about a hole in the ground which had a flight of broken steps leading down into it; four of them were at the bottom and the remaining two crouched at the top, listening to what was being said downstairs. Spelmann's shout attracted their attention; they stood up and peered through a screen of tall weeds. Then one of them spoke to his friends below.

"Something funny going on up here," he said. "Two men chasing each other."

The four men came up. "Anything on top here," said one, "would be funnier than what's down there. What is it?"

"It's that comic private detective grandpa we had pointed out to us in the square. He's chasing somebody. Look out, they're coming this way."

Spelmann had told Hambledon that a battalion could be concealed in that area of desolation. He was quite right; the six men simply disappeared from sight, only to lift their heads again after Fitzner, followed by Spelmann, had passed by.

"One of 'em's vanished," said a commentator in a clump of willow herb. "Our collaborator has lost him. He's casting about. He's stopped. He's going on slowly. Now he's disappeared too."

They waited a few minutes but saw no more, and the leader of the party rose to his feet. "They may have found something," he said. "We'll go and see, I think."

They walked across to the place where Spelmann was last seen and found a stairway leading downwards behind a wall. They listened, and a voice floated up to them. "Fitzner," it said. "Herr Fitzner. I want to ask you something."

"Halt, in the name of the Reich," said one of the grinning policemen, and they filed down the uneven steps. At the bottom they found themselves in a series of cellars opening one out of the other and reasonably clear of obstructions; the inspector in charge went on, torch in hand, until he came to a right-angled turn. He switched the torch off and put his head round the corner.

"There's a light showing further on," he said. "Somebody moving about with a torch."

The narrow cellar they were in ended in a doorway, with the door still on its hinges and pushed right back against the wall. They passed through the doorway to find themselves in a large room at the far end of which was the short but wide figure of a man carrying a very small electric torch with a failing battery. He turned the feeble beam towards them and said: "Who are you?"

The inspector turned his own torch upon Spelmann and answered that they were police.

"Glad to meet you. I am Heinrich Spelmann. I followed a man down here, but I've missed him in the dark. My torch battery——"

He was interrupted by a sound from the doorway by which they had entered, and the inspector swung round, torch in hand. The door behind them had shut with a dull thud.

"Hi!" shouted the inspector. "What are you playing at? Open that door, one of you."

One of them did his best to obey, but the door was quite immovable and had no handle on the inside. Further examination showed that it was made of steel.

"Looks to me," said another, "like the door of a safe, the inside of one. It is, look. This deep doorway here was a big safe once, and somebody's cut the back out of it to get through to here."

"The man you were chasing," said the inspector, "must have been hiding behind the door against the wall outside. I suppose this is a joke," he added rather doubtfully.

"His name is Fitzner, Ritter Fitzner," said Spelmann, "and if he's what I think he is, the joke will probably be in what is rightly called very bad taste."

There was a moment's pause while this remark sank into the minds of his hearers.

"You take the situation with commendable calmness," said the inspector. "Is there another way out of this room?"

"Possibly," said Spelmann, "possibly. If there is, we shall find it. May I ask if anybody knows where you gentlemen were going this afternoon?"

"Only that we were going to have a general look round. We are not actually on duty at the moment."

One of the police who had been poking about said that the place was unexpectedly clean and that the walls and ceiling had been whitewashed.

"Ah," said Spelmann. "If this is the room in which they held their meetings, there should be electric light available unless, of course, Fitzner has thrown the main——"

The inspector turned his torch towards the door; one of

the police leaped at a wall switch thereby revealed and turned it down. The room was brilliantly lit by a lamp at the far end; it was indeed pleasantly clean and tidy. In the far corner the top of a trestle table leaned against the wall with its folded legs beside it; a dozen or more chairs were neatly stacked near by with a rolled carpet laid across them.

"This was the conference room, evidently," said Spelmann. "I had heard a description of it. We shall not, at least, lack the means of resting our legs when we are tired." He drew out a chair for himself and sat down upon it.

The inspector personally directed his men in a search for some other exit. The search, which included tapping the walls and roof, took some time because it was very thoroughly done, but it was entirely barren of result; as for the door, an oxyacetylene cutter might have had some effect on it, but nothing that they could improvise did more than scratch the enamel in places. Eventually the police stood back and looked to their inspector for further suggestions. The inspector walked across to Spelmann, who had pulled out a second chair to rest his feet on.

"You will forgive my idling like this," he said. "I have had some extremely tiring days and I was sure that your excellent men would search for another outlet much more efficiently than I could."

The inspector begged him not to mention it, and Spelmann said that he understood there was a ventilating shaft somewhere with an electric fan in it which was kept running when there were many people in the room.

"We found the shaft in that corner," said the inspector. "It is six inches square in section. We have not found any other switch which might operate it; there is only the light switch by the door," and Spelmann said that the fan switch was probably somewhere outside.

The inspector drew out a chair for himself, sat down upon it, and said: "Tell me. What do you really think that young man had in mind when he enticed you down here? Just to lock you up for a few hours?"

Spelmann's bushy eyebrows went up. "I think I have annoyed them very much," he said, "and by 'them' I mean the organization called the Silver Ghosts. You are the special police from Bonn, are you not, who have come here on their account? Yes, I thought so; I saw you in the square this morning."

"Up to now," said the inspector ruefully, "they seem to have accounted for us."

"They think I know too much, especially after the girl Sophie came to me for protection. They are quite right, I do. So I expect they thought it unsafe to go on using this room for meetings, and since they don't want it any more and it has a nice strong door, I imagine it looked like a safe and easy way of getting rid of me—permanently."

"Do you mean to say that the idea is to leave us here to die?"

"Me," said Spelmann, "not 'us.' I shouldn't think they'd dare do that to six policemen. You see, they didn't try to trap you, did they?"

"No," said the inspector bitterly. "No, we just walked into it like a—like an——"

"Like an issue of bonus shares," said Spelmann courteously.

"Then you think that when they've laughed themselves silly about us they'll come and let us out?"

"Don't you?" said Spelmann.

The inspector looked at him, got up abruptly from his chair, and went to tell his men to take turns in shouting up the ventilator shaft. "It must communicate with the outer air," he said. "Somebody might hear us."

So for the next half-hour a steady stream of "*Hilf! Hilf!*" —Help! Help!—flowed up the ventilator shaft in a variety of masculine tones, until the men began to cough and remark that shouting made one thirsty and there didn't seem to be any water laid on. Spelmann took to prowling round the room, looking intently at everything from a cobweb in the corner to a stout hook in the ceiling, the sight of which appeared to affect him unpleasantly. He was staring at the lamp when a sudden thought struck him; he dragged out his watch and looked at it, asking at the same moment for the exact time.

"Twenty-three and a half minutes after twenty-one hours," said the inspector. "Why?"

"Just in time," said Spelmann, making a dash for the electric-light switch and proceeding to switch it on and off. Three shorts, three longs, three shorts. Three shorts, three longs, three shorts. Three shorts——

"Must you do that?" said one of the policemen. "You're making my head ache."

"It's S O S in the Morse code," said another, "but what's the good? Nobody can see it."

"No," said Spelmann jerkily between clicks, "but they can hear us. There's a Peter-car goes down the Grosse Budengasse—just at the end here—between half-past twenty-one hours and a quarter before twenty-two hours every night, and he's got a short-wave transmitter-receiver on board——" Click-click, click-click, click-click.

174

"Do you really think he'll pick up the effect of that little switch going on and off?"

"I don't know, but I hope so. Where did I get to? Oh yes ——" Click-click. "I know he—picks up neon—signs and the like of—that. He'll hear an S O S if it's—ever so faint; he was —a wireless operator at sea——" Click-click.

"I think you're right," said another policeman. "I did a term of duty in a Peter-car last year, and we used to pick up all an' sundry if they weren't fitted with suppressors, which practically nothing was."

Spelmann carried on, patiently clicking while the time crawled slowly past, until the inspector said the time was just on ten and if the Peter-car was going to hear them it had already done so, surely.

"I'd better keep on," said Spelmann, changing hands for the tenth time. "Makes your arm ache. They'll be able to tell if they're getting nearer, won't they?"

"Excuse me," said another man who had not previously spoken, "but why don't you tell him where we are?"

"What, in Morse?"

"Yes, of course."

"I'm sorry," said Spelmann, turning slowly red, "but this is the only Morse I know, S O S."

"Let me have a go, then. I was a wireless operator once."

"Why in the name of heaven," said the irritated Spelmann, "couldn't you say so before instead of leaving me to do it all?"

"Didn't like to butt in," muttered the man. The flashing was interrupted for a minute or two while Spelmann and the inspector drafted a message.

"Shut in below ground about fifteen yards south Unter

Goldschmied near Laurenzplatz stop cannot receive only transmit stop find stairs down behind wall leading to cellars stop steel door probably resembling safe stop."

"There," said the inspector, giving the written note to the ex-wireless operator. "Keep on sending that till I tell you to stop. Herr Spelmann, come and sit down. You there, bring a chair for the Herr."

Spelmann, moving with well-earned dignity, sat down.

The time dragged slowly on; eleven o'clock, midnight. At a quarter past midnight the overworked lamp bulb suddenly gave out and they were left in the dark. The ex-wireless operator left off clicking the switch.

"Go on, go on," said the inspector. "You know that message by heart by now, surely."

"Yes, sir. But with a broken bulb in the lamp there's no electrical circuit, so there won't be any message going out."

"Oh, surely," said the inspector. "It isn't as though the switch had gone. Every time you work it you make or break a connection in a line carrying electricity, don't you?"

"No, sir, not really. You have to make and break a circuit to produce an electric impulse such as can be picked up by a short-wave wireless receiver."

"Sounds odd to me," said the inspector. "You other radio experts present, do you agree?"

There did not appear to be any other radio experts present until the man who had done duty with a police car raised a diffident voice to say that of course you didn't get interference from neon lights unless they were switched on; they didn't do it all the time by just being there, as it were.

"Of course they don't," growled the ex-wireless operator.

"Let's get this straight," said the inspector. "You say that

neon signs give out signals—well, electric impulses, then—
all the time they're switched on. But nobody's switching
them on and off all the time, are they?"

"Yes, sir, in a sense. They are——"

"What d'you mean, 'in a sense'?"

Spelmann, realizing that tempers were getting heated,
put his tactful oar into the troubled waters.

"In my opinion, if I may put it forward," he said, "the
question of whether we are now transmitting or not is
probably academic. If the Peter-car didn't pick up the S O S
before ten I don't suppose anyone has heard any of it. If
they did pick it up they must be as sick of hearing that
message as you are of sending it. They would have located
us by now."

"Then why aren't they attacking the door?" asked the
inspector.

"They may have been playing with the lock for the past
two hours," said Spelmann; "we shouldn't hear them. That
door's probably nine inches thick."

"Then what will they do?"

"Dig us out, I hope. If they've found the door they'll
know where we are."

Some time passed before one policeman remarked to another that it was a pity Prick-ear was in the "cooler," and
another man laughed and said, "They can get him out, can't
they?"

"Who is Prick-ear?" asked Spelmann.

"A safebreaker, sir. He's a wizard with locks, especially
the kind with letters or numbers instead of a key. He turns
the dial and listens, and they say you can see his ears wig-
gling."

More time passed and a man said: "Oh dear," and yawned audibly, which set the others off, as it always does.

"Lie down, men," said the inspector evenly. "Lie down on the floor and take it easy." He switched on his torch for a moment to see that they all obeyed.

"Oxygen going," said Spelmann in a tone lower than a breath, and the inspector nodded.

More time passed till Spelmann sat up sharply because he thought he heard a noise. The others heard it, too, for one man said "Listen," and most of them moved slightly. The sound came again and again, a steady thump-thump-thump, very slow, at about two-second intervals.

"That's them," said one man, and his voice cracked with relief as he spoke.

"Digging with picks," agreed another, "an' not far off, either."

"*Nun danket alle Gott,*" said another, and the inspector said: "Amen. Sing it, boys, sing it."

So they sang, not loud, and rather breathlessly, the ancient German hymn which is in English "Now Thank We All Our God." A quarter of an hour later the first pick point broke through the roof, bringing down a scatter of stones, a gush of fresh air, and a shaft of early daylight. The men retired hastily from beneath it, shouting encouragement to the diggers, but the inspector bent anxiously over Spelmann, who was stretched out upon the floor, taking no notice.

"Poor old chap, has he fainted?"

One of the policemen had been a medical orderly during the war; he felt Spelmann's pulse and touched his forehead.

"Fainted, nothing," he said cheerfully. "He's asleep."

And so he was. When the hole in the roof was big enough to pass the body of a man, they had to wake him up to tell him so.

Spelmann's first enquiry when he was once more aboveground was for the present whereabouts of Ritter Fitzner.

"What? Old Otto Fitzner's son, the cinema owner? He's dead."

"Nonsense," said Spelmann, repressing a crawling sensation down his spine, "nonsense. He was alive yesterday evening."

"So he was, yes. But he was run over by a car at the Neue Brücke crossing last night and killed outright."

Spelmann sat down heavily upon a fallen column, and somebody sensibly gave him some cognac.

"So now we shall never know," said the inspector, sitting down beside him, "whether all that was a joke or not. After you with that flask."

Forgan and Campbell climbed into the autobus when it called for them at the Dom Hotel that morning and took their seats. The other members of the party were all men and all Germans—the bus was not quite full—there were fifteen altogether. The guide, whose business it was to keep the party together during the tour and to tell them about places of interest en route, evidently realized from their accent that Forgan and Campbell were strangers and made himself particularly pleasant; the other passengers were extremely friendly, and the modelmakers settled down to a thoroughly jolly afternoon. The Allied Commission's head-quarters at Bonn came in for some light badinage since Spain is not there represented; Beuel afforded an oppor-tunity for getting together over a glass of beer; by the time the bus reached Eberjagen the members of the party might have known each other for years.

Eberjagen consists of one hotel, half a dozen small houses, and a tiny church; the road here runs along a shelf on the hillside so that the houses are not so much on either side of the road as above and below it. The hotel was a pleasant white-painted building of the chalet type; steep gables had deer's antlers fastened at their peaks, and there was a beautiful iron lantern hanging from a bracket at the corner of the house. The hills in this district are covered with pine trees; the hotel stood in a little clearing of its own with a gravelled car-park in front; behind it the ground fell away sharply so that it was obvious that the rooms at the back must have one or more storeys below what was ground level in front. Very useful, no doubt, for cellarage and storage. The air was fresh and pine-scented; a small stream crossed the road by a culvert to fall in a series of cascades to the Rhine a mile away and nearly a thousand feet below.

The guide said that here they would stop for half an hour to permit the passengers to stretch their legs and obtain refreshment in the hotel. They would find the accommodation to be everything that the most exacting traveller could require. Forgan and Campbell, who were by this time the friends of all the world, were delighted with the place and said so. "Half an hour," said Campbell, "isn't nearly long enough. I should like to stop here for a week."

The guide laughed and said he'd better speak to the landlord about it; the landlord, a burly man smiling in the doorway, said that the house was theirs and everything in it, and the whole party jostled happily together into the inn. The first room was large and scrupulously clean with small tables covered with blue-and-white-checked cloths having wooden chairs set about them. Forgan turned towards the right, but the guide touched him on the arm and said: "Through here, if the Herr pleases. There is a room at the back reserved for this party."

Forgan nodded and walked, with Campbell at his heels, down a short passage with closed doors on either hand to a room at the end with the sun streaming in at the windows and lying in golden pools on the polished floor. Four men of the party followed them; the door at the far end of the passage closed audibly and then the door of the room they were in. Campbell, who had walked across to the window to look out, turned sharply, but it was too late. A sudden pain at the side of his head, a sensation of falling immense distances into blackness, and he knew no more until he awoke to find himself in a small room with walls some eight feet high. The door was composed of very solid bars and was plainly locked; light came through the bars from outside.

Campbell moved his head and winced; opened his eyes, tried to focus them, and shut them again. He was lying on a mattress on the floor—— Forgan, where was——

"D'Almeida, my friend," said Forgan's voice, speaking Spanish. "D'Almeida, here am I, Piccione." He was naturally afraid lest Campbell in the first shock of waking should speak English. "How is it with you?"

"I have the headache," answered Campbell in Spanish; "it hurts to open my eyes." He did so nonetheless and saw Forgan sitting upon another mattress opposite. "Where are we?"

"I think they mistake us for Daniel and put us in the lion's den," said Forgan. "Behold the bars."

There was the sound of movement outside their cell, and Campbell realized that they had an audience who might possibly understand Spanish.

"And you, Piccione? Did the big cat scratch you also?"

"I have a bump on the head, that is all."

"I am thirsty," said Campbell, changing to German. "I want some water. Are they Christians here, do you suppose?"

"I shouldn't think so," said Forgan in the same tongue, "but we can try. Oh, *Kellner!*"

"*Kellners* only supply beer," said Campbell.

"Coffee would do. Hi, *Ober!*"

A man came to the barred door and looked in at them; it was Hugo Geisel, who had called at their hotel and taken them to meet Volkenborn at the Excelsior, and they recognized him at once.

"Be quiet," he said. "You can have coffee. Wait in silence."

He went away and came back ten minutes later with mugs of steaming coffee which he put down upon the floor. He then took a revolver out of one pocket and a key out of another and unlocked the door. Still with the gun in one hand, he moved first one mug of coffee inside the cell door and then the other and relocked the door.

"One would think," said Forgan, removing the mugs, "that the little man was afraid of us."

"Someone—thank you, Piccione—has told him that we bite. I don't bite, do you, Piccione?"

"Only nice things," said Forgan, and tasted his coffee. "You know, D'Almeida, I can't help thinking I've seen that man somewhere before."

Geisel moved away out of sight.

"You are right, as usual," said Campbell; "he is the boot-boy at our hotel."

"No, no. He is the lavatory attendant at Cologne Station."

"Surely not. That man washed behind the ears, I noticed it particularly."

Geisel came back, white with anger.

"This insolence will not serve you," he said. "Wait till tomorrow, and we will teach you to be polite."

"What, you underbred warty-nosed scrofulous little bit of dreg," said Forgan, "do you want to turn the Spanish Government against you? You cheap scullion, *remember whom we hold as hostages.*"

This was an arrow at a venture, but it sank to the feather. Geisel gasped, turned on his heel, and walked quickly away; a moment later they heard a door shut.

"That shook him," said Forgan, sitting beside Campbell on his mattress and speaking into his ear.

"What were you referring to? That story about Hitler living in a village near Cádiz? I think it's nonsense; Hitler's as dead as the Pharaohs."

"I think so, too, but there's somebody there, obviously. I mean, in Spain."

"Dozens of 'em," said Campbell. "They weren't all killed by a long chalk, the top-ranking Nazis. Nor all tried at Nuremburg. If they can't get to the Argentine, where else would they be?"

"I wonder how long it will take Hambledon to find out where we are."

"He's missed us already," said Campbell, looking at his watch. "It's half-past nine."

"Do you suppose all those men on the bus were in this swindle?"

Campbell nodded mournfully. "They seemed such nice people, too. Weren't we mugs?"

The night passed without incident, though they did not sleep particularly well. With the morning came breakfast, coffee and rolls brought by the innkeeper protected by Geisel with a gun; the Englishmen only knew that it was morning by their watches, since no daylight reached that place and the electric light was on all the time. No words were spoken by either side, and presently the door out of sight closed again and they were left alone.

"They don't mean to starve us, anyway," said Forgan. "These rolls are quite good. What is all this about, do you know?"

"Unless they're going through our things for those papers we couldn't find."

"If they find them I suppose they'll release us with apologies, will they?"

"Then I hope they're better searchers than we are," said Campbell emphatically. "And the apologies will have to be something special too."

The whole day passed without incident, and though the prisoners asked questions, demanded release, and delivered insults calculated to send blood to the head of a white mouse, they received no satisfaction at all. Geisel and the innkeeper took it in turns to guard and attend to them and obstinately refused to speak.

Late at night, at nearly midnight, the prisoners were disturbed by the unseen door opening and the sound of two men's voices. They sat up and listened and then rose to their feet to look through the bars of the door, but the bars were thick and close together, it was not possible to see far to either hand.

"Now we shall see," said a German voice in a tone of satisfaction. "We will this tangle unriddle."

"Careful," said another voice, "one of them——" And the words became inaudible.

"I know, I know. Why don't they come?"

There followed the sound of footsteps and several more voices speaking; the last was high-pitched and aggrieved and spoke with a vile Spanish accent.

"I demand an explanation of this so-unheard-of outrage," it said. "I, Alfonso Demetrio d'Almeida y Monstrelet, a gentleman of Spain, demand——"

Forgan and Campbell turned their heads and looked at each other.

"Gird up your loins, brother," murmured Forgan, and Campbell gave his trousers a nautical hitch. "The *Luz de la Luna* must have been jet-propelled," he said.

Geisel came to their door, unlocked it, and said: "Come out." The Englishmen strolled past him as though he were not there and saw for the first time the place in which they were held: a wide passage with cells like theirs down one side, three of them, a concrete floor sloped to carry off water to a drain at the end where there had once been an entrance, now bricked up, and one door at the side opposite to the cells.

"I have it," said Forgan to Campbell. "Stables."

"Or cowsheds. You're Buttercup and I'm Cowslip."

They both laughed and went on towards the far end where there was a table and chairs and a group of men standing about who turned and stared at them as they came. Two of them were the Spaniards they had met in Paris; a third was Gustav Volkenborn, apparently in charge of the proceedings.

"Look," said Forgan loudly, speaking German, "the burglars from Buenos Aires."

"We are not!" yelled D'Almeida. "It is you who are robbers and cheats——"

"Really, gentlemen," said Campbell, addressing the Germans, "rather a noisy meeting, is it not?"

"You will all be silent and hear me," said Volkenborn. "Two of you are the Herren d'Almeida and Piccione, the other two are impostors. We shall now establish which is which. The genuine Herren will receive our explanations and apologies, the impostors will be most savagely punished. Now then. You," addressing D'Almeida, "your story."

D'Almeida drew himself up and said with considerable dignity that he had already told them his story twice but that if a third repetition would enable them to grasp it at last he would be happy to oblige. Campbell nearly applauded. D'Almeida then gave a brief and quite accurate account of what had happened in Paris so far as he understood it, though naturally much of it remained an unsolved mystery to him, how the stolen jewellery came to be found in their rooms at the Ambassador, for example. Finally he said that they left the ship at Las Palmas when she put in there for supplies, obtained help from friends who lived there, and went by air to Cologne to repair, at the earliest possible moment, whatever damage had been done to the cause by the incredible outrage which had been committed upon their persons. He added that he and his friend were prepared to make excuses for the natural confusion in the minds of their German friends, but that this unpardonable discourtesy would cease forthwith. He would hear their apologies and he and his friend would decide whether or not they were acceptable. He then glared round him at everyone present, drew up a chair, and sat down.

It was quite obvious that D'Almeida's statement made a good impression on the Germans; its sincerity was patent and the mere fact that many of its incidents were ridiculous and humiliating told in its favour. No man would make up such a story against himself. Volkenborn said, "Thank you," and turned his hard stare upon Campbell.

"I must congratulate my impersonator," said Campbell blandly, "upon quite the most ingenious story I have ever heard. He should write thrillers, he has the *métier*. I cannot compete, I admit it frankly. I would but ask, where are his proofs? His wild and beautiful story holds me enthralled but it does not convince me in spite of the supreme art"—he bowed to D'Almeida—"of its telling. For ourselves, we can only offer dull and prosaic proofs. We entered Germany quite openly; we carry our own passports duly stamped with the Military Permit of Entry of the Allied Commission. We have brought with us such documents as we were told to bring and the sum of twenty thousand German marks. We were only awaiting the production of some mutually acceptable proofs of identity such as we were promised at a certain meeting on Thursday night"—he looked at Volkenborn—"to hand over these things and conclude our business. Instead of which"—he drew a long breath and his voice rose—"we are decoyed away by a vile trick, sandbagged, locked up in a disused stable for a night and a day, and treated with the grossest discourtesy by the mannerless lout you left to attend us. I say that if this is how you treat messengers, if you prefer fairy stories to proof, if you act with violence instead of courtesy"—he banged the table under Volkenborn's nose—"I say that you are not the sort of persons with whom a Spanish gentleman can be expected to deal and that I shall advise my friends to have nothing more to do with you." He dragged a chair noisily across the floor and sat down upon it.

Forgan remarked in a mild voice that he agreed with every word which his distingushed compatriot had uttered, and Piccione, who had not spoken at all until then, said that the Caballero d'Almeida had spoken only what was in his own heart also. Then they all sat down and looked coldly at Volkenborn.

The German said that it was merely a question of proofs, and Campbell immediately broke in to say that was the mistake from the outset and that he had said so before leaving Spain. "Some form of mutual recognition—I repeat, *mutual* —should have been arranged beforehand. This system by which we arrived blindfold in Cologne to wait to be picked up like a parcel was not only insulting but ridiculous."

"I associate myself with that," said D'Almeida firmly. "For all the inconvenience caused to us"—he spoke directly to Volkenborn—"you alone are to blame. This affair was mismanaged from the start."

"The distinguished caballero," said Campbell with a bow to D'Almeida, "will, I hope, accept my thanks for his timely concurrence."

D'Almeida nearly bowed in return, recollected himself, and stared blankly at the opposite wall.

Volkenborn reddened with anger and was about to speak when one of the men who stood behind his chair leaned forward and whispered in his ear. He listened and nodded.

"There is an easy way in which to prove which of you is right," he said. "These papers for which we asked—I do not speak of the money—they were concealed in your luggage.

You will both tell me where they were hidden and we will go and see if what you say is true."

"They are not there now," said Campbell; "they are in the hotel safe."

"Yes, but where were they?" asked Volkenborn. "There are almost certainly traces of where such papers had been hidden."

D'Almeida leaned forward, his face alight. "They are in a travelling toilet case in my suitcase. It is a flat leather case about twelve inches by eight with a zip fastener running round three sides. The case contains hairbrushes, razors, and so on, and is lined with watered silk. The papers are underneath the silk lining, between that and the leather. They may, as this fellow says, have been taken out and put elsewhere, but there must be a considerable cut in the lining."

Volkenborn nodded and said: "Thank you, gentlemen. I must ask you to accept our hospitality, such as it is, for a few hours longer while someone goes to the Dom Hotel to see if the travelling-case lining has been cut. Or even," he added with his eyes on Campbell, "not cut. I wish you good night, gentlemen."

He walked towards the door leading out of the place. D'Almeida and Piccione made to follow him but were stopped and told that they must stay there.

"What," said D'Almeida furiously, "and sleep in these miserable cow stalls?"

"Why," asked Piccione, "does all this have to happen to us?"

"Uncivilized brutes, these Germans," said Campbell affably.

The next day passed without incident until just after eleven at night, when once more the door opened and footsteps and voices were heard.

"These people," said Campbell in a bored voice, "always hold their social gatherings in the middle of the night. When do they sleep?"

"They don't," said Forgan, "their consciences won't let them."

He was interrupted by an angry voice in German telling somebody to "Go in there," and another voice with an unmistakable English accent saying "Go to hell." There followed the sound of blows, a woman cried out, and a door clanged shut and was audibly locked.

"Another time," continued the German voice, "obey me at once."

"That's Volkenborn," said Forgan, nearly dislocating his nose in an effort to see sideways through the bars, "but who's the lady?"

"Magda von Bergen," said Volkenborn, like an answer, "you have been brought here under suspicion of betraying the cause. If you cannot clear yourself you know what will happen, don't you? There is a hook in the ceiling up there, look at it."

"Opposite us, look," whispered Campbell, "just up there. What does——"

"It does not matter what answers I make," said Magda's voice, clear and steady, "I am sure you will hang me afterwards to cover up your own sins."

"It does matter what answers you make," said Volkenborn. "It is not the thought of hanging that need trouble you but what is going to happen to you first."

"Let her alone," yelled a voice in English and changed to German. "If you hurt her I'll——"

"That must be that fellow Yeoman," said Forgan, under cover of the rest of the sentence. "I don't like the look of things, do you?"

"Ernst," said Volkenborn, "take her."

"That's the innkeeper, blast his filthy soul," said Campbell, and D'Almeida broke in in a high angry voice.

"Do not dare to touch the lady! You bestial fiend——"

"Quiet," snarled Volkenborn, "or it will be the worse for her. One word out of any of you and I'll break her arm. Now then, Magda, dear Magda. What did you tell that Englishman?"

"I told him to go away and never come back."

"That is true," said Yeoman eagerly.

Magda cried out suddenly and Volkenborn said: "That's your doing. I told you not to speak. Go on, Magda. What else did you tell him?"

"He wanted me to go to England with him and I said I would not."

"Go on."

"I—we kept on arguing like that——"

"Go on."

"There wasn't anything more, only the same thing over and over again. I couldn't get him to go away; you would not have me call the police?"

"Fool," said Volkenborn, "idiot, why didn't you call us?"

"Because I didn't want—to disturb you."

"Liar. It was because you didn't want us to find him. What did you tell him about us?"

"What does it matter," cried Magda, "since you are going to kill us both?"

"So you did tell him about us——"

"But you caught us at once; he had no time to tell anyone else——"

"This time, yes. But how much had you told him before?"

"Nothing—nothing—nothing. Aa-aah!"

"I can't stand much more of this," said Campbell, with the perspiration running down his face.

"Nor I," said Forgan.

"Bring her here," said Volkenborn. There was a momentary shuffling sound and then a scream that made their ears ring. The place filled with a babel of sound, George Yeoman shouting like a madman and rattling the bars of his cell, D'Almeida and Piccione yelling in Spanish, and Magda sobbing aloud.

"Silence!" bellowed Volkenborn, and a hush fell like a blow. "Now, Magda. Those alleged Spaniards went to your room the day before the meeting. Why did you not report it?"

"I was afraid you would be angry about it and the deal would not go through."

"I see. You think you know better than I what is best for the cause, so you keep me in ignorance of what goes on. Well, let that pass, you won't have a chance to do it again. Now, what did you tell them?"

"Nothing. They didn't ask me anything. They walked in without knocking and scolded me because they had been kept waiting in Cologne."

"Kept waiting, and by whom?"

"By the person they were expecting to meet."

"And why did they think you knew anything about the person they were expecting to meet?"

"I don't know. I haven't the least idea."

"You haven't the least idea. Out of all the streets, houses, rooms, and garrets in all Cologne, they have to come to your street, your house, your room, and they are strangers to the place. How did they know where you lived?"

"I don't know, I——"

"Because you told them, that's why. They are spies and you are a traitor. Bring her here——"

"Oh no, no, don't——"

"Hi!" shouted Campbell at the top of his voice. "Hi, Volkenborn! Stop torturing that girl. We'll talk."

"So you'll talk, will you?" said Volkenborn. "And who told you my name? This slut here?"

"No," said Campbell. "A policeman, actually. We saw you one day after meeting you at the Excelsior, you remember? So we said to a policeman, 'Who's that?' and he said you were the gallant and distinguished Herr Gustav Volkenborn of the Volkenborn Rheinische Schiffahrtsgesellschaft. So when you were introduced at that meeting as Fritz Rückseite, we hardly knew where to look, as they say."

"Not Rückseite, surely," said Forgan. "Wasn't it Rülpsen?"

Both these words, though harmless in themselves, are definitely rude when applied to a person, and Volkenborn was beside himself with fury. He snatched the door keys from Ernst, the innkeeper, and strode towards the cell with Ernst hurrying behind, counselling caution, care, "there were two of these men and——"

194

"Now I see him I remember," cried Campbell triumphantly. "The name was Räudig," which means "mangy."

Volkenborn tore open the cell door and rushed at him; the innkeeper, to do him justice, followed in to help. Magda leaped at the door of Yeoman's prison and clung to him through the bars; D'Almeida and Piccione at the far end alternately called upon their saints and appealed for silence to hear what was happening, but all that could be heard was a confused noise of battle which gradually died away. There was silence for a long minute and then Campbell's voice, rather breathless.

"I do believe," it said, "that mine's dead."

"Mine too," said Forgan cheerfully.

## 15 GOOSE FOR CHRISTMAS

Forgan took the keys which had been left in his door and released the other prisoners; Magda von Bergen was in a state of collapse so that there was no getting any information out of George Yeoman. When asked how one got out of that place he merely said: "What? Pass me that water jug. Anybody got a clean handkerchief?"

"One idea at a time, that fellow," said Forgan. "What a householder he'll make; can't you see him laying the stair carpet? 'Pass me the hammer.'"

The Spaniards D'Almeida and Piccione were genuinely horrified and concerned about the lady; they dragged mattresses out of cells and tore their coats off to cover her. Campbell waited until D'Almeida became inactive for a moment and then approached him.

"By favour, señor, a word with you."

"Certainly, señor."

"It is idle to deny that there are matters of difference between us, but I hope sincerely to gain your agreement when I suggest that we bury them for the time being. We are in the hands of cruel enemies, señor, and there is the lady to consider——"

"Señor, for the time being we are allies," said D'Almeida

196

warmly. "You and your friend are men of courage and re-
source and we will not look beyond that for the moment.
Later we will speak of——"

"Certainly," said Campbell. "Now, we were unconscious
when we were brought here. How does one get out? Is that
door the only exit, and where does it lead?"

"A short passage and a steep ladder at the end which
leads up to a trap door in the innkeeper's office. There was
a carpet over it when we arrived; it was turned back and the
trap lifted."

"Many people in the hotel when you came through?"

"Only the innkeeper and that fellow Geisel."

"I wonder if he is up there now," said Campbell. "A trap
door is a nasty thing to force against opposition. I must ask
Yeoman. I say, Yeoman, just a moment."

"What? It's all right, Magda, I'm here. I won't leave
you."

"Yeoman," said Campbell patiently. "Yeoman, Yeoman,
Yeoman——"

"Did you want me?" said Yeoman, looking up.

"Did I w—— Listen, Yeoman. We've got to get the lady
out of this."

"Of course. At once. She——"

"When you were brought here tonight, were there many
people about in the hotel above here?"

Yeoman thought for a moment.

"There were the people who came with us, but I heard
Volkenborn telling them to go on."

"Go on where?"

"I don't know. I was anxious about Magda and wasn't
really listening."

Campbell sighed. "Didn't you gather whether it was some distance away or merely upstairs?"

"Oh yes. He told them to take the Mercedes."

"So there isn't a car outside now, I suppose?"

"Oh yes, there's the Maybach. We came in two cars, she in one and I in the other. She——"

"Yes, yes. So all the men went away except Volkenborn and—anybody else?"

"They all went away except Volkenborn. There were two men already here, the one you killed and another; his name was something like Geiger."

"Geisel, probably. He remained upstairs, did he? He didn't come down——"

"No. He stayed by the trap door. Magda, you're looking better. Try to drink this water."

"If we can get upstairs we'll find her something better than water. I remember a bar in that front room. I say, Forgan."

Forgan came along from what had been their prison. "It is abominable to rob the dead, but there are plenty of fireworks where they've gone," he said, and offered Campbell the choice of two revolvers.

"Thank you. There is a steep ladder and a trap door which, when last seen, was occupied by Geisel. This way."

They opened the door and saw at once, in the light falling from an upper room, a steel ladder upright against the end of the passage and a trap door standing open above it. They shut the door behind them and crept quietly along the passage.

"No legs dangling," whispered Campbell. "No shadow cast by the form of a patient sentry."

"Perhaps he's gone to bed," murmured Forgan. "It is, after all, nearly two in the morning."

"I'll go first," said Campbell. "I've got rubber soles." He went up a few steps and listened intently, went up a few more and put his head out, went up the rest and crawled out on his hands and knees into a tiny office not much larger than a cupboard. Forgan followed up the ladder, and Campbell, keeping his head close to the floor, looked out into the passage. A head near the floor is much less conspicuous than one at the usual height; besides, it may be mistaken for the cat.

"Nobody about so far," he said, and stood up. He was in the passage down which they had walked on the day they arrived; to his right was the room in which they had been attacked, to his left the big lounge across the front of the house, the bar, the front door, and freedom. There was no light visible in the house except the one left burning in the office, but someone had left an electric torch on the office desk and Forgan took it. They explored the ground floor in a few minutes; there was nobody about.

"Geisel has gone to bed," said Forgan.

"I see no need to wake him," said Campbell. "It isn't getting-up time yet. Or he may have gone home."

"What, in the Maybach?" said Forgan, and very quietly unfastened the front door. "No, she's there all right, good."

"Perhaps he has a bicycle, like the man in that film we saw. Shall we have a look round outside? How nice the woods smell. Put your light out, there's a car coming."

They flattened themselves in a shadowed angle of the house, but the car swept on without pausing.

"What's in here?" said Forgan at the door of a small shed.

"Not locked, honest people about here—look, Campbell."

"Petrol. Gallons of it, all in cans. I say, Forgan, we have
——"

"Two corpses to dispose of. I was thinking about that. Do we burn the place down?"

"Much simpler than facing the police on a murder charge. Let's get the others out and get on with it."

Ten minutes later Magda was in the big Maybach car with Yeoman helping her to champagne in a thick glass. The Spaniards had raided the bar and found three magnums, which they opened by knocking the tops off. Forgan and Campbell, laden with jerricans of petrol, snatched a drink in passing, and the Spaniards, tired, nervous, and excited, finished it up. It is an exhilarating drink and it did them good. At the end of the third magnum they felt quite splendid and had forgotten everything Forgan had said about being quiet. He and Campbell were down in the basement room arranging a funeral pyre for Volkenborn and Ernst with a special view to destroying any evidence that they had been throttled.

"Piccione," said D'Almeida, "we are discourteous and neglectful. We have not enquired after the lady for at least half an hour."

"You must do the talking," said Piccione. "For some reason I cannot, at the moment, remember the German for 'how is your health?' "

They went out to the car, but, though their enquiries were both elegant and sympathetic, it became plain in less than five minutes that Magda and Yeoman preferred to be alone. D'Almeida, as soon as he realized this, said that, difficult as it was to tear themselves from the company of the most charming señorita, they had promised to help their friends inside. They wandered in at the front door, across the lounge and into the passage, noticing with surprise that the trap in the office floor was now shut.

"Can they, then, have already finished?" began D'Almeida, when there was a flash, a loud report, and a bullet hit D'Almeida in the left arm. They swung round as Geisel fired again and missed Piccione, who uttered a scream of rage and sprang at him. D'Almeida immediately joined in and they all fell to the floor, struggling and panting, until the battle ended in D'Almeida's hitting Geisel on the head with a doorstop and then holding him down while Piccione produced a large clasp knife from his pocket, opened it, and carefully cut the German's throat.

They got up gasping and only then realized that the trap door was being banged and heaved from below to the accompaniment of choking yells, also that every time the trap lifted an inch smoke poured out of it. They tore the trap door open and pulled out Forgan, who staggered two steps and fell flat on top of the German. D'Almeida said: "The other, the other," and dropped down the ladder; between them they dragged out Campbell just in time, as the draught reached the fire below and with a roar the whole underground passage was alight and a flourish of flames leaped out of the opening. Campbell and Forgan, though blinded and choked, were not unconscious; led by the Spaniards, they staggered out of the hotel and were pushed into the back of the waiting car. Piccione got into the driving seat with D'Almeida, nursing his arm, beside him; started up the car and went off down the hill fast and then faster as the great car gathered speed. Piccione could drive indeed, but he did not know the road; he took the first bend much too fast and nearly left the road. There was a loud squeal from the tyres as the Maybach skidded, just missed the opposite bank, straightened out, and roared away into the night. Behind them there was a glow between the trees, a flicker, and then a glare of flame tossing and leaping against the dark.

Spelmann, after the unpleasant night with the police in the cellars of the Unter Goldschmied, was tired out and went straight to bed. Six hours later he woke up and no amount of telling himself to go to sleep again availed in the slightest against the overactivity of his anxious brain. He got up and went to his office.

No doubt last night's events had improved his standing in the eyes of the police, but he knew perfectly well that it was his demeanour under stress which had impressed them and not his cleverness. In fact, apart from that one brilliant idea about the electric-light switch, he had been rather conspicuously stupid, walking open-eyed into a simple trap like that, though it was a consolation that the police couldn't afford to say so since they had walked into it after him like a string of sheep trotting innocently after an old ram. He writhed as he thought of it. There was Sophie, too, poor Sophie, who had put herself under his protection and been snatched away as easily as taking a rattle from an inattentive baby. Not good enough, not nearly good enough. He stood at the window of his office looking down into the street and seeking for inspiration. "I am to be a great detective," he told himself. "I know it, I feel it here," and he laid his hand upon his diaphragm. "Nevertheless, now that I am entrusted with the solving of this so great mystery of the disappearing Spaniards, what can I do? An idea, *lieber Gott*, an idea, *bitte*."

No idea came, and he sat down to read the *Rheinische Zeitung*, Cologne's daily paper. There was a small news item at the bottom of a column which attracted his notice. The paragraph was headed: "Fire at a Country Hotel" and ran:

> In the early hours of yesterday morning the hotel at Eberjagen in the Siebengebirge was totally destroyed by fire. The fire was not observed until the hotel, a wooden building, was alight from ground to roof. It is feared that there was some loss of life, as three bodies were discovered among the ruins. The cause of the fire is not known. The hotel is well known to tourists, as it was one of the regular stops for autobus tours to the beauty spots of the Siebengebirge.

Spelmann read the paragraph twice. On the face of it there was nothing to connect it with his case except that it was one of the hotels—the last, in fact—at which Autobus BR 87208 had called upon the trip from which Forgan and Campbell did not return, and hotels do catch fire occasionally, especially wooden ones. He told himself that he was chasing shadows and read the leader page without taking in a word of it. He turned back to the paragraph and read it again.

"I shall not be happy if I do not look into this," he decided. "If it is all a mare's-nest I need not tell the Herr Hambledon."

He went to Bonn, hired a bicycle, and rode to Eberjagen. The hotel was completely burned out; the fire must have been very fierce because all that remained of it was a low heap of wood ash with some bathroom fittings, blackened and cracked, sticking out of it and, at the back, a long rectangular hole in the ground.

"Cellars, no doubt," said Spelmann, and scrambled down the bank to look more closely. There were some odd iron objects which looked like short lengths of high railings with very thick bars. They were not sections of railings, for they had locks on them; they were doors, or gates. The sort of thing behind which wild animals are kept. Very odd. Those three bodies, now . . .

He remounted his bicycle and rode slowly along the road to the nearest house, which was a quarter of a mile away. There was an old man leaning over the gate and Spelmann dismounted.

"Nasty fire you've had here."

"Yes," said the old man, "yes, and I were the first as saw it. I weren't asleep, look, an' I heard a big car come down like the devil was after it, and just on the bend 'ere—you see this bend just beyond 'ere—there was a squealin' and a screechin' and I thinks, Lord, they've crashed. So I gets up and looks out of window and there was a glow all among they trees there. That was the hotel, all on fire!"

"Good gracious," said Spelmann, "must have startled you."

"It did, it did. So I gets into my trousers and a coat and I goes off up road to call some'un of my neighbours, for I lives all alone 'ere, look. Well, I'm lame, look, and it's all of half a mile to Hoffmann's house and all uphill. Well, when I passed hotel I could see 'tweren't no good, fire was comin' out of top windows then. Still, Hoffmann, he comes and two-three others, but we couldn't do aught but stand an' watch it burn. Didn't see nobody, but when they pulled over the ashes in the morning there was three on 'em, all burnt to cinders and shrivelled up no bigger than monkeys, oh dear, oh dear, and Ernst Muller, he was a fine big man."

"Dreadful," said Spelmann, "dreadful. Who was Ernst Muller? The landlord? I think I remember him."

"Yes, the landlord. They reckon one was him, though they couldn't recognize him, and another they reckon was a man been staying with him this past week, Geisel or some such name. Who the third was maybe nobody'll ever know."

Spelmann was very interested by the mention of Geisel, but his face did not change and all he said was: "What an experience for you! It is fortunate that there were no more people in the house."

"There was more people earlier on because there was a big black car stood outside quite late, my daughter told me —she passed by about midnight, she'd been with Frau Goertz, who's lying-in. A big black car, she said, but they must've gone off earlier; 'twasn't there when I passed the fire. That was, what, getting on half-past two, I reckon."

"Is your daughter here?"

"She's in the house now; she comes in to cook me dinner and that. She don't live 'ere, she's married. Lives up the road."

"I've got some friends touring here in a big black saloon car," said Spelmann. "I've been trying to find them; we've missed each other somehow. I wondered whether——"

"She wouldn't know one car from another. Still, you can ask her. Martha! Gentleman wants to know something."

Martha came out, but her father was only too right. A car

to her was a big black one or a small blue one or a long green one or an autobus, but you wouldn't call that a car. She was very sorry.

Spelmann thanked them and rode away towards Bonn, passing on the bend a long spectacular skid mark which reached right across the road. That car had certainly been travelling. Now he came to think of it, there had been a big black Maybach saloon standing outside the hotel on the day when he was enquiring about the mystery autobus. Only the day before yesterday; it seemed longer ago than that. All these disappearances and excitements, they do stretch out time.

He picked up, here and there, news of the black car being furiously driven through the night. A man sitting up with a sick cow near Honnef came out for a breath of fresh air and saw it pass; a group of young people from a dance at Godesberg leaped for the side of the road as it roared by, and one of them said it was a Maybach. Near Wesseling a doctor's chauffeur, waiting outside a house of sickness for his master, was startled out of a doze when it missed him by inches.

"Going to Cologne," said Spelmann, and pedalled on.

At Köln-Deutz he sought out a policeman he knew and said: "Were you on duty the night before last? . . . You were? Did you see a black Maybach saloon being driven very fast, coming from Bonn, at about a quarter or half-past three?"

The policeman said, with emphasis, that he did. He was at the road junction when such a car came at about that time. "At the last moment, Herr Spelmann, they decide to take the Bergisch-Gladbach road and they come round in a skid; *Herr Gott*, I am almost killed. I leap for it and fall; when I rise to my knees the taillight disappears down the road. If I had his number I would teach him something! You are detecting some important crime, are you?" he added, suppressing a grin, for Spelmann's activities had not been very highly rated among the Cologne police.

"I am looking into a small matter," said Spelmann with dignity.

"Well, if you detect the number of that car for me I'll tell you where you can buy a goose next Christmas."

"Thank you, thank you," said Spelmann, hopping to re-mount his cycle.

"But if you're chasing an erring wife you'll want something faster than that," said the policeman. "At the rate they were going they'll be in Italy before this."

Spelmann waved his hand and pedalled off towards Bergisch-Gladbach. Of course, supposing that the missing friends of Herr Hambledon—and the other Spaniards—and, possibly, Magda and her Englishman—were hidden away at Eberjagen, there was no proof that they had escaped. They might be dead and he pursuing the Silver Ghosts, a terrifying thought. But there weren't enough bodies for all of the missing men. But perhaps they weren't all there. Perhaps they had never been there; it was only the old man's mention of the name Geisel which made him so certain he was on the right track; there might be other Geisels and Spelmann had had enough experience to know what an exasperating nuisance Coincidence can be when she tries.

He made a few enquiries as he went along, but nobody had seen or heard the Maybach. Presently, only a mile or so short of Bergisch-Gladbach, he heard a story about a car in a pond and turned aside to ask about it. The pond was down a narrow and steep lane; when the farmer came past it he found that there was a car in it. They were dragging it out with a tractor and Spelmann saw it slowly emerge.

It was a black Maybach saloon, and there was nobody in it, nor had anyone floated out, since the doors were shut and the windows but slightly open. It had been pushed into the pond to conceal it.

Spelmann sat down upon a bank, lit a cigarette, and thought this over. Either the car's occupants had gone on somewhere else by some other means of transport, possibly the tram, or they were staying somewhere in the neighbourhood. More likely the latter, since if they were by now far away, why push the car into the pond? They might just as well have left it beside the road. The attempt to hide it suggested that they were not far away.

Spelmann realized that he was hungry; it was past midday, he had had a lot of exercise since breakfast, and it should therefore be possible to combine business with pleasure. He rode on until he found a café, where he had beer and a fricandelle—a sort of rissole—but they had no visitors staying there. At another he had more beer and fricandelle but no information; at a third, beer but still no news. He rode on, telling himself that he had guessed wrong and might as well go home. He would try just one more.

The fourth place was a small hotel with one big room for dancing tacked on at the side; it stood back from the road in an isolated spot; one wondered where the dancers would come from. Spelmann rode up twenty yards of rough track and entered the bar.

The landlord was sullen and grumpy in manner and

served Spelmann's beer as though he begrudged it. To Spelmann's cheerful enquiries as to whether he ever put up visitors he said no. He hadn't the accommodation, and anyway, there was enough to do without bothering with visitors. Spelmann was just about to write this place off as another blank when a woman, presumably the landlord's wife, came in and spoke to him in a low tone. He nodded, picked up a brass tray, put six glasses on it, and handed it to her.

This intrigued Spelmann. "It is curious," he said, "to set out six glasses on a tray if you have no visitors, is it not? Or is it perhaps that you and your wife have palates so fine that you must have each refill out of a clean glass?"

The landlord scowled and told him to mind his own business. Spelmann ignored the rudeness and said that, on the contrary, it was his business. He was, he said, riding about trying to locate some friends who were staying somewhere in that district, and it looked as if he had found them.

The landlord, thus pressed, said unwillingly that he had got some people staying there, he didn't want them, they had forced themselves upon him, and that Spelmann could go in and see them if he liked, if only to arrange for them to go somewhere else. The landlord then opened a door leading to a short passage with another door in it obviously admitting to the dance hall.

At the very last moment the thought that this party might, after all, be the Silver Ghosts recurred unpleasantly to Spelmann's mind and he hung upon his heel for a moment. Then he straightened his back and walked in.

There were six people sitting there round two small tables pushed together; Magda and her Englishman, the Spaniards who were Hambledon's friends, and two other men, doubtless the other missing Spaniards. Spelmann stopped just inside the closed door, bowing low, his long white hair curved forward like the crest of a cockatoo, and within him his heart was singing.

"*Gnädiges Fräulein*," he began, "*gnädige Herren*. Heinrich Spelmann, private detective, at present in the good service of the Herr Hambledon."

Campbell sprang to his feet and said that the most excellent Herr Spelmann was as welcome as flowers in May, in fact, more so, and how did he find them?

"Mein Herr, I was told to find you and I have done so. As for 'how,' we detectives must have our little secrets. I will but say that had a certain pond been deeper I might not have found you so quickly."

"I remember you," said Forgan. "On the day that the late Geisel called to take us to see the late Volkenborn you were sitting first in the entrance hall of the Dom Hotel and later in the lounge of the Excelsior."

"At the Herr Hambledon's desire."

"Exactly, he told us so. Magda, this is Hambledon's pet sleuth, Herr Spelmann; Herr Yeoman, Herr Bonamour, Herr Cierra. Come and sit down and have something."

"Thank you, no, I have been tracing you with beer, as it were, and at the moment—no, I thank you, no more. I will sit with you, if I may, for a few minutes and then I return to the Herr Hambledon, who sits upon nettles until he has news of you."

"We are anxious to get into touch with him," said Campbell, "but the telephone here is out of order and we think we shall live longer and more happily if we are not seen in Cologne. Tell him we are here, will you, and that we have a good deal to tell him?"

"Certainly, certainly. He will doubtless come here. May I ask one or two unimportant questions which you will not, of course, answer unless you wish. First, did I hear you refer to the late Geisel and the late Volkenborn? They died in the fire, did they?"

"A little before, actually," said Forgan. "The fire was an afterthought."

"That Geisel," said the smaller of the two Spaniards, "I cut his throat and my name is Piccione, not Cierra."

"Now don't start that again just now," said Forgan, "you'll muddle the Herr Detective," and indeed Spelmann looked puzzled enough. "All shall be explained in due time to come. Another question?"

"To the *gnädiges* Fräulein von Bergen. You have with you—upstairs, perhaps—the Fräulein Sophie Maeder?"

Magda leaned forward eagerly. "No, I have not. She isn't here; I thought she got away?"

"She did, Fräulein. She came to me, but she was lost

afterwards. You have not seen her? I hoped when I saw you that she was with you."

Magda shook her head slowly and tears came to her eyes. Spelmann rose to go; he was indeed anxious to astonish Hambledon at the earliest possible moment, but she stopped him.

"Herr Spelmann, would you do something for me or ask the Herr Hambledon to do so? I would not trouble you, but indeed it is important."

"Tell me, Fräulein," said Spelmann, sitting down again. "I am entirely at your service."

"I have a room in the Schildergasse," she said, and gave him the address and room number. "There is a sealed envelope in my room which might help us all if I could have it. It is old and faded because it has been sealed up for seven years; the seal on the back is an eagle holding a cross. It is—remember this—it is behind the right-hand top drawer in my chest of drawers. Pull the drawer right out and you will find the envelope stuck on the back of it with adhesive tape. If you could—but I expect the house is watched—do not trust the doorkeeper——"

"Let your heart be at peace," said Spelmann simply. "If it is still there you shall have it."

"Ah, if it is still there——"

"I go at once," said Spelmann, and went.

On his way through Köln-Deutz he met again his friend the policeman.

"Well," he said, "did you overtake the eloping lady?"

"No," said Spelmann sadly, "you were right. They have escaped to Italy."

He cycled on over the new bridge and straight to the

Gürzenich Hotel, where he found Hambledon just returned from Bonn. Tommy took one look at Spelmann's face and said: "Come up to my room."

Spelmann poured out his news like a tide and Hambledon's congratulations were unfeigned. "I must go and see them," he said, "but I can't go tonight, I'm expecting a telephone call later on. In the meantime we'll go to that apartment house in the Schildergasse and get the Fräulein Magda's letter for her. Then if you'd take it to her, if you're not too tired—you have had an immensely long day already——"

"Mein Herr, in such a cause I would work also all tonight, though indeed I think I will go by tram and not by bicycle this time. The calves of the legs, you understand. In a tram one sits. It is but a short walk from the tramline at the other end."

"Go by any means you please," laughed Hambledon, whose sense of relief was such that he would have laughed at anything. "A tram—hire an autocycle—buy a donkey—borrow an invalid chair, so long as you get there. Now let's stroll along to the Schildergasse. I'll get the doorkeeper to show me a room preferably on the top floor; that'll exercise my calves also, as there's no lift. As soon as you see the coast is clear you slip in and do your stuff. Can you unlock the door?"

"The gracious Fräulein lent me her key," said Spelmann, "and even if she had not, we detectives——"

"Oh, quite," said Tommy. " 'Stone walls do not a prison make, Nor iron bars a cage,' eh? You'll clear off as soon as you've got it, don't wait for me. Tell them I'll be there tomorrow morning soon after nine, and in the meantime they are to lie low and not let anyone see them. All right? By the way, the finding of that car will have to be hushed up, I'll see to that."

"If the letter is no longer there," said Spelmann, "I will wait for you in the street outside."

"Yes, do. But I think it will be; the local Silver Ghosts have had enough on their plates these last forty-eight hours without ransacking the Fräulein's room on the off chance of finding something they don't know is there. I mean, they probably will search her room on principle, but I should think tomorrow would do for them. Or even next week. Well, good night, Spelmann, and once again, damned well done! You wait here and I'll tackle Cerebos. I mean Cerberus. See you tomorrow."

The envelope was still there with the red seal of the eagle holding a cross still unbroken. Spelmann walked unchallenged out of the house and caught the tram to Bergisch-Gladbach.

Hambledon went to Bergisch-Gladbach in the morning by a circuitous route which ended in his walking the last few miles from Bensberg, which was on a different tram route. He found them all still there, safe and well, which agreeably surprised him, since if Spelmann could track them down surely the Silver Ghosts could do so. Perhaps they thought that all their prisoners had died in the fire at Eberjagen; it was devoutly to be hoped that they did.

"But what made you pick on this place?" he asked.

"Purely fortuitous," said Forgan. "We ran out of petrol, so we alighted and looked round for somewhere to hide the car. The pond was not entirely successful; either it wasn't deep enough or the Maybach was too high. We did

hope that nobody would go and look at it for a couple of
days. Why did somebody have to? Haven't they got anything better to do than walk round looking at ponds, or did
it happen to coincide with the annual visit of the Herr
Regional-derelict-ponds-Inspector?"

"It was the farmer," explained Hambledon. "His cow
wanted a drink. But you needn't worry about the car; it is
now locked up in a shed and no word of its being found will
appear in any newspaper, police notice, or other public
print."

"We pushed the car down the lane while Magda steered,"
said Yeoman. "It was rather fun."

"Then we walked on and eventually saw a light. It was
then about 4 A.M.," said Campbell, "so we went to see what
it was all about, detaining Magda in case it was something
which required expurgating. But it was only our landlord
filling up white-wine bottles out of a cask full of something
which smelled of rotten apples. We observed this easily because the shutters were not correctly adjusted. We then
retired upon Magda, who said he could go to jail for that,
and rightly. Not only 'could' but 'should,' in our opinion."

"So we all went and knocked at his door," said Forgan.
"We had to knock because it was bolted. He came to the
door eventually, giving a spirited rendering of a poor man
unwillingly dragged from a deep sleep. He said so. So we
said we thought he'd like to know that there was a kobold
in his kitchen filling up wine bottles with rotten-apple cider
and what would the police say if somebody rumbled it?"

"He told us to go away," said Magda, "but Herr Campbell told him that we were the only witnesses to his innocence, so he'd better let us in."

"We told him that if he sent us away," said Forgan, "he would be sure to get into trouble with the police and only we could save him."

"We pointed out," said Campbell, "that it's no good pleading kobolds-in-the-kitchen without at least six witnesses. So he let us in and here we are."

"May I say," said D'Almeida, "that I and my friend are disgusted with Silver Ghosts? We should like to return home."

"If we could take our money with us," said Piccione, "we can report that we were so dissatisfied that we broke off negotiations."

"I say, Hambledon," said Campbell in English, "could you do something for these poor mutts? They have had a rough trip all through, and there's no doubt they saved our lives at Eberjagen. We've become quite fond of them these last two days."

"I'll think it over," said Hambledon. "I don't know that they'd better go yet. When they get home they'll talk, naturally, and we don't want news getting back here again before everything's cleared up, whenever that may be."

"Herr Hambledon," said Magda, "may I say something?"

"Let us retire to the other end of the room, shall we?"

She nodded and walked to the far end of the hall with Hambledon beside her and Yeoman following behind.

"Will you believe me when I say that I joined this organization because I believed that they would work for a better Germany? Now I see that they have all the bad features of Nazism back again, the bullying, the lying, the brutalities and murders, the secret tribunals. I was very stupid and credulous; I even believed that those two young men had hanged themselves out of remorse for so nearly betraying us. I say now that all this must be ended and now that the hope is false——" She stopped suddenly.

"I had one piece of news this morning, Fräulein," said Hambledon.

"What was that?"

"The Fräulein Sophie Maeder. I am sorry, Fräulein. Her body was taken out of the Rhine this morning."

"Drowned?"

"No, Fräulein. Not drowned. Let it go at that."

Magda von Bergen turned so white that Hambledon thought she was going to faint; she closed her eyes, crossed herself, and he saw her lips move.

"Why did you have to tell her that?" whispered Yeoman furiously. "Hasn't she endured——"

"Be quiet," said Hambledon abruptly.

Magda opened her eyes and looked at him steadily, and Hambledon met her eyes for a long moment.

"I believe you, Fräulein," he said. "You will help us to wreck this horrible——"

"If it's the last thing I ever do in this life," she said, and crossed herself again.

"I think you were about to suggest something," said Hambledon.

"Yes. I will tell you. Arrangements were made in case the Cologne branch of the Silver Ghosts was ever raided or broken up. A meeting will be held in a lonely house in the woods not far from Wermelskirchen. It will be attended by various leaders from other places; I don't know who they all are. They will reorganize the branch. The meeting will be summoned by an advertisement in the *Rheinische Zei-*

*tung*, in the personal column. It will be worded: 'Hans. Meet me on'—whatever the date is—'without fail. Franz.' We must look out for it, but I don't know if I can get the paper here——"

"Never mind," said Hambledon. "I'll see that it is not missed. It won't appear for some days, I suppose?"

"It will take a few days to arrange it," she agreed. "When it takes place——"

"We will round them all up," said Hambledon.

"I shall attend it," said Magda firmly.

"Oh no, you won't," began Yeoman, and Hambledon said he didn't think so, either, but she stopped them both.

"Listen. I've been to this house before and I know where it is. There will be a ring of sentries in the woods all round it. When I arrive, not too early so that most of them will already have arrived, one of the outposts will take me in. That will leave a gap through which you can follow, capture the other outposts in silence, and surround the house. I shall be glad if you can get there in time to hear what I have to say."

"But——" began Hambledon.

"You see," she said, "those who have joined the Silver Ghosts are not all brutal and vile; indeed, Herr Hambledon, indeed they are not. Many of them are fools like me who follow the hope they have been shown. I have something to tell them which will make them give up that hope, and the party will collapse—being without a hope." She smiled sadly, and Hambledon asked her why, if she knew their hopes were vain, she had supported them so long.

"Because I didn't know until last night when I opened the letter the good Spelmann brought me. My father was a doctor and he was concerned in the generals' conspiracy to assassinate Hitler, only he was never found out. But he was always afraid it would come out sooner or later, perhaps after he was dead; there must be several men still alive who know that he was in it. Then, if the Nazis rose again, they might turn on me. So he showed me this envelope and told me that after he died I was to take it and keep it unopened till I was in danger. He made me swear not to open it except in case of need, for then it might save me."

"Well?" said Hambledon.

"He died and I hid it away. Last night I opened it."

"Well?"

"I think it may save not only me but any other innocent dupes. So I am going to the meeting."

"I don't like it," said Hambledon doubtfully. "I think you are taking a risk."

"Not so much as you think. I am a party member, I have a right to attend and to speak. Besides"—her voice dropped—"I led Sophie into this. If I can save even one life in exchange, I might someday be able to forgive myself."

There was a short pause, and then Hambledon told her that the meeting place in the Unter Goldschmied had been found. "I think it will be opened up or closed down or both," he said. "I don't think those cellars are wholesome, morally or hygienically."

"They are not," agreed Magda, "they are horrible. We broke through from one to another and at last we came to a huge safe built into a wall and we got the door open. There was nothing in it, but we thought it would make a very good front door. So we cut through the back of the safe and found quite a large room behind. We tidied it up and whitewashed the walls and got some chairs and a table down there; it made a very good meeting place and the electric light was still working. Extraordinary, wasn't it? We used to meet there to draft resolutions and correspond with other branches. We composed leaflets, got them secretly printed, and distributed them, all that sort of thing. Delegates from other places used to come and address us, and we all felt very brave and busy and important."

"It all sounds great fun," said Hambledon.

"It was, really, until Volkenborn's father died and he came home to manage the business. I don't know where he'd been since the war, but he was recommended to us as an important man among the Silver Ghosts. In fact, he was appointed Gauleiter for the Cologne area whether we liked it or not, and after that it was all different. More efficient, of course, but oh, he was a brute," she added passionately, "and I'm glad he's dead!"

"Yes," said Hambledon. "I think we do very well without the Herr Volkenborn. There was a Herr Lotz, too, was there not?"

"Herr Lotz," she said quickly, "was shot one night when he attacked George outside his house, and no one knows who did it."

Hambledon blinked, and George Yeoman said innocently that he supposed somebody chose that moment to pay off some old score. Evidently Yeoman was not to know the true story; perhaps Magda thought he might consider it unmaidenly.

"One more question if I may, Fräulein. Mentioning no names, do you know who Herr Heintz is?"

Magda smiled and nodded. "He has been living at Bonn

for nearly a year," she said. "He isn't a university professor, but there are several—how do you put it?—private ones—extramural is the word, I think. They have some particular subject in which they take private pupils, and he was one who did that. Chinese history was his subject."

"He'll be at the Wermelskirchen meeting, I suppose?" said Hambledon. "He's not living at Bonn now. Gone away, leaving no address."

"Then I don't know where he is," said Magda, "but I expect he'll be at the meeting if possible."

Hambledon nodded and rose to go. "Señores," he said, addressing D'Almeida and Piccione, "I go to arrange if possible for your happy return to your own country. The money in the hotel safe is a problem in itself; the management will certainly refuse to give it to me or to you either, and I don't intend taking my friends into Cologne at the risk of their lives in order to get it out for you."

Their faces fell. "Señor," said D'Almeida, "with respect, we wish to return home at once. This place does not amuse us and we are not even comfortable. The beds——"

"I am sorry," said Hambledon, "but what do you suppose I can do about it here and now?"

"You can accompany us on the tram to Cologne," said D'Almeida firmly. "You can go with us to the Dom Hotel and inform the manager that your friends were impostors and we are the real owners of the money. It will then be paid out to us; we can collect our luggage and leave Germany this afternoon, preferably by air."

"Señores," said Hambledon, "there is no doubt that the Dom Hotel, like all the others, including mine, is watched by the Silver Ghosts. If we do that I shall have to come out in the open and our chance of abolishing this gang will vanish."

"Señor," said D'Almeida, "it is true that we detest this gang and all its works, but let me point out to you that they may be your responsibility but they are certainly not ours. Spain, not being a member of the United Nations," he said pointedly, "has no share in the government of Germany. I speak for Piccione as well as myself when I say that we have been your cats'-paws long enough in this business. We suffered enough loss and humiliation in Paris, to say nothing of our treatment on that ship, to deter us from lifting a finger to help you any more. We combined with the gentlemen whose names, I believe, are Campbell and Forgan to get this lady and ourselves out of that horrible place, but now that you have come here I understand that their troubles are over. I would add that even our treatment by the Silver Ghosts was their fault; if they had not impersonated us we should have had no difficulty. I say again, señor, we have suffered enough at your hands. Get us our money, please, and our luggage, and we will go home."

"I'm sorry you take that line," said Hambledon. "You force me to tell you frankly that, sooner than let you go home now and tell your story where it can be sent back again to the gang here, I will chain you up in the cellars under this place with an armed guard over you until I see fit to release you. Or shoot you out of hand, whichever you prefer."

"This is an outrage," began D'Almeida, but Hambledon cut him short.

"You yourselves are not so innocent as you make out. You were conspiring to promote this intrigue which you

knew perfectly well was illegal and was organized and
headed by Nazi war criminals harboured by your government. You entered this country on passports not your own,
for which the Allied Commission could imprison you, quite
apart from the subversive purpose for which you came. You
also broke about a dozen currency regulations. I can have
you conveyed to Paris, where the police will no doubt be
happy to start you again upon your journey to Buenos Aires,
or you can go straight home and tell your friends that you
have lost their money and all their confidential papers, besides making a laughingstock of yourselves and those you
represent. Well?"

There was a full minute of complete silence broken at
last by Piccione. "What I want to know," he said in an aggrieved voice, "is, why should all this happen to us?"

"Because you pushed your way into a game too rough for
such as you," said Hambledon.

"Señor, you are insulting," said D'Almeida.

"It is the truth which insults you, not me. If you hadn't
made fools of yourselves in Paris——"

"We should have had to think up something else," said
Forgan.

"You made it too easy," said Campbell. "I hate having
to say it after what you did for us at Eberjagen, but you
had to be stopped and we were going to do it one way or
another."

"Are you all members of British Intelligence?" asked
D'Almeida.

"No, no," said Forgan. "Dear me, no. We just do it for
a hobby."

D'Almeida's jaw dropped, Piccione attracted the attention of his patron saint to what he called "this morbiferous dissipation," and Campbell laughed.

"Brother," he said, "you ain't seen nothing yet. So far we've only been playing with you."

"Playing," repeated D'Almeida blankly.

"Listen," said Hambledon, "and don't let's go all grim about it. You have had a very unpleasant time and I'm very sorry about it, but you brought it on yourselves, didn't you? All I'm asking you to do is to stay here quietly with the others for a very few days to let us finish off the job, and then we'll get your things out of the hotel and you shall return home with dignity and honour. If you will give me your parole to stay here and not try to escape I will promise in return to get you away as soon as I possibly can or at least find you somewhere more comfortable to stay. Well?"

"Very well," said D'Almeida. "You have my word of honour."

"And mine also," said Piccione.

"Stout fellow," said Campbell, clapping him upon the shoulder. "I'll tell you what I'll do to make the time pass pleasantly, I'll teach you to play poker. Hambledon, a pack of cards, please?"

"I'll send some up," said Hambledon, suppressing a laugh. "I'm sure you will all enjoy it."

## 17  THE HOUSE IN THE WOODS

East of Wermelskirchen there is wooded, hilly country, small rounded hills densely covered with forest. It is only thinly populated; the scattered villages are tiny, consisting of thirty or forty houses, two or three shops, a post office, and a church, which often has an onion-shaped spire running up to a point as thin as a lance. A few forest roads run through the woods, which are, for the most part, as remote and lonely today as they were six hundred years ago.

Most of this country is taken up by large estates, each centring upon the Schloss So-and-so, vast lonely castles once filled with patriarchal families and innumerable servants, now three-parts empty and desolate with perhaps three or four elderly relations huddled together in one wing for company and waited on by ancient servants as stiff-necked as themselves. The Schloss Rensburg was one of the most remote, deep in a hidden valley full of the sound of falling water. Two ladies lived there, both childless widows, the Baroness Alberich von Rensburg and her sister-in-law, the Baroness Sigmund von Rensburg. Baron Alberich had been the elder brother, so his widow Hildegarde, though only fifty-six, took precedence over Baron Sigmund's widow Mathilde, who was over seventy. They had each a small suite of rooms wherein they spent their days, meeting only at mealtimes in the great dining room.

The Baroness Hildegarde, who had once been beautiful, was a hard-faced, weather-beaten woman who was out and about all day trying rather hopelessly to keep the estate going until the return of the present baron, a nephew and a prisoner in the hands of the Russians, if he were still alive. They had had no news of him for over two years.

Still further back in the woods and nearly four miles from the castle there was what was called the hunting lodge, a small stone-built house of one enormous sitting room, a kitchen, and four bedrooms above. It had been built a hundred years earlier to provide shelter in case of bad weather, or merely as a place for meals, for the vast shooting parties given by the Baron Alberich's grandfather. A forester and his wife lived there now, and sometimes the Baroness Hildegarde rode over on her pony to look for broken windows or leaks in the steep roof of small thick grey slates. The forester's wife would curtsey, shoo the children out of the way, and offer the baroness bread and cheese and milk; the forester would remain standing, cap in hand, all the time that she was in the house, and go down on one knee to provide her with a mounting block when she got into the saddle again.

On several previous occasions men had come secretly in the late evening to the hunting lodge; the forester and his fellows had had little sleep on those nights; by the baroness's orders they had patrolled the rides which converged upon the lodge like spokes in a wheel. The baroness had not attended the meetings, though she had paid several visits to the lodge on preceding days and consignments of

food and wine had been conveyed there from the castle.
The Baroness Hildegarde said nothing about it to the
Baroness Mathilde, but they never had a great deal to say
to each other at any time.

Late in the evening of the day when Denton was fired
at in the café in Bonn, the forester from the lodge came in
haste to the Schloss Rensburg and spoke privately to his
mistress. She sent a message by her maid to the Baroness
Mathilde saying that she had a headache and was going to
dine quietly off a tray in her own rooms and go to bed early.
Another message brought the saddled pony to the side door
and ten minutes later the Baroness Hildegarde ran quietly
down the stairs, mounted him, and rode away on the edge
of the grass.

When she came to the hunting lodge she saw a small
black saloon car drawn up at the door. The forester's wife
came out and led the pony away while the baroness tapped
at the door of the big sitting room. A voice answered; she
opened the door and dropped a low curtsey upon the thresh-
old.

Martin Bormann rose to his feet as she came in, but it
was not towards him that the baroness was looking.

Four days after the burning of the hotel at Eberjagen a
notice appeared in the *Rheinische Zeitung* imploring Hans
to meet Franz on the following day at twenty-three hours,
which is 11 P.M. No meeting place was mentioned; evidently Hans was expected to know it. Hambledon, who had
already been to see Magda again with the largest-scale map
of the Wermelskirchen district which Bonn could provide,

also knew where it was, but only Magda had been there before.

"It is here, in the middle of this green patch," she had said, with one slim finger on the map. "It is said to be 'near Wermelskirchen' because that is the postal address of the Schloss Rensburg, but the hunting lodge itself is actually nearer Dhünn, and the nearest station is Wipperfürth, here. When I was there before we went by train to Wipperfürth and were met by a car which took us a couple of miles along this road; it goes to Wermelskirchen and Remscheid ultimately. After that the car turned left into a narrow lane for another nearly two miles, I should think, and then we got out and walked quite a long way along grass rides cut through the woods. It was very lovely there."

"I see," said Hambledon. "You didn't actually go to the Schloss Rensburg at all."

"Oh no, that was much further on. No, I've never even seen it."

Armed with this information, Hambledon went to Bonn, where his story was heard with the most enthralled interest. The Intelligence Office called conferences which were attended not only by Security people but by quite high-ranking Army officers. "I haven't mixed in such distinguished society for years," Hambledon told Denton. "Who is the horribly handsome general who comes and coos in my left ear? I wish he wouldn't, it tickles."

"The Baroness Hildegarde von Rensburg was a terrific Hitler fan," said Denton, "so a casual eye is cast upon the Schloss Rensburg from time to time."

"Is there no baron?" asked Hambledon.

"She had a son in the Luftwaffe who was shot down over

England and subsequently died in Canada. I understand the *de jure* baron is a Russian prisoner, poor devil."

When, therefore, the expected advertisement appeared it set in motion something like a military operation. Since it was desired to collect the Silver Ghosts, not scatter them, the actual surrounding of the house was timed for a quarter to midnight. Long before that hour lorries filled with troops came by circuitous routes to converge upon the Rensburg woods and decant their passengers in the gathering darkness at the outer ends of the woodland rides. But before this, an hour earlier at least, several interesting things happened.

Magda von Bergen, riding a bicycle, came up the road from Wipperfürth soon after ten-thirty and turned into a rough cart track leading through the woods. She saw and heard nothing, but there were men in the woods who travelled almost as fast as she could ride that rough and rutted lane. In fact, where in extra-bad patches she had to dismount and walk, they had to hang back not to get ahead of her.

A mile along the lane a light flashed at the bicycle and a voice halted her. She got off at once and showed something she carried, which was examined by the light of the torch which had flashed the warning. Her credentials were evidently satisfactory, for the man waved her on and stepped back into the bushes, where large hands closed over his mouth and round his throat. He was lifted from the ground and carried away.

"Do they all show lights like that?" somebody asked in a hoarse whisper, and another whisper said that apparently they wanted to see her badge.

"It's a shame to take the money," said the first voice, and was shushed into silence.

The next stop occurred at the point where Magda must leave the lane for the woodland ride. She asked the man on guard whether it was any use taking her bicycle any further, to which he replied that she could please herself but she wouldn't be able to ride it. So she propped it against a tree, asking as she did so whether there was anyone further on who would show her the way.

"Two more between here and the house," said the man helpfully, for which the stalkers in the woods thanked him in silence. "We hand you on from one to the other," he added. "Stand aside a minute."

She moved aside and the man pointed his torch up the ride and showed two long flashes, after which she walked briskly on.

When this man also had been silently collected the officer in charge of the party suggested that it might be a good idea to use the signal to guarantee the following party. "We should get right up to him that way, shouldn't we?"

"I don't think you'd better," said Hambledon. "They are probably counting their visitors and she may be the last. She is very nearly late."

The officer nodded. "We are doing very nicely as we are," he said.

Magda hurried on; she was using her bicycle lamp to see her way and the next sentry hardly delayed her. The last was standing where the ride ended in the clearing in which the house stood; six rides met here and there was a man stationed at each of them. When she had gone up to the door of the house these six men signalled to each other with torches and came together for a few minutes. Hambledon was quite right; they had been counting their visitors and the tally was complete.

They talked in low tones for a few minutes and then returned to their posts. If the sky is clear the nights of midsummer are never really dark, but beneath those black pine trees the darkness was dense indeed. One by one the men melted into the shadows and disappeared completely; one would have said that they were no longer there.

"Now," said the officer, "get a move on. We've got to mop up the blighters in all the other alleys before the stubborn an' heavy-footed infantry move in. Shift, you wall-eyed cripples, shift!"

Hambledon, left alone, crept quietly up to the house. There were windows at intervals the whole length of the big room; they had outside shutters over them, but the night was very hot, so the shutters were set ajar and the windows were open behind them. Tommy selected one which had a bush against it, in case some member of the party should come out upon the doorstep for a breath of fresh air. Hambledon leaned against the wall, rested his elbow comfortably upon the window sill, and listened.

Inside the room the meeting was under way. Somebody was thanking the chairman for his introductory remarks and then getting down to business. He regretted having to tell those who had not already heard the news that their good comrade Gustav Volkenborn, Gauleiter of Cologne, had lost his life in a fire at a hotel in the Siebengebirge where he was spending the night, and with him had perished Party Member Hugo Geisel and also their faithful adherent Ernst

Muller, the landlord. It was one of those tragedies etc., etc. The most effective way of mourning their colleagues was to replace them as soon as possible in order that their work might go on.

"Who the devil's this nattering?" Hambledon asked himself, and shifted about to try to see into the room. But there were curtains inside the window, and the most he could see was a narrow vertical strip of somebody's coat sleeve.

"There is a temporary hitch in the arrangements for transferring money from Spain," continued the speaker, "but the matter is well in hand and a satisfactory conclusion may shortly be expected."

"If Magda can keep her face straight at that she's got no sense of humour—please God," said Hambledon fervently. "Very dull, this fellow."

But the speech brightened after that, as though the speaker had got the dull business part over and was now able to unburden his heart. Their future task was so to build the foundations of the party that when the time came—he could see it not so far off—when war with Russia broke out and the Western Powers had their hands full and overfull, the party could take over from the spineless time-serving incompetents at Bonn, those truckling lackeys of the Allied Commission, and make their dear Germany once more a Great Power. There followed a sentence which puzzled Hambledon completely. "Then," said the speaker, "you will see your Hope come forward openly in the face of the whole world"—he was interrupted by applause—"great and glorious, no longer cherished secretly and, as it were, under tutelage, but come to full strength and wisdom, no longer a

Hope but a splendid certainty, to lead the people to a final victory."

"That's an odd way," thought Hambledon, "to talk about hope. By the way, Magda said some——"

The chairman asked if anyone had anything to say, and Magda, outwardly calm if her knees were unsteady, rose from her seat near the door.

"Magda von Bergen, party member. I have something I should like to say to the meeting."

"Come to the table, *gnädiges* Fräulein von Bergen."

The table referred to was a long narrow one placed across the top of the room; all the chairs faced it. There were three people already at the table: the chairman, who was the same Herr Muller who had conducted the Cologne meeting; on his left hand Martin Bormann, still dishevelled about the head but wearing a tidy lounge suit and no spectacles; and on the chairman's right hand in the place of honour a boy of about fifteen. The boy had dark brown hair, unruly hair which would never be tidy for long; a heavy lock of it fell forwards over his forehead. He had dark eyes in a thin, eager face; his features were good and his expression intelligent. He was at the coltish age, when arms and legs seem too long to be quite under their owner's control and tend to become twisted round chair legs or lash out in unguarded moments and kick things. At the moment he looked a little apprehensive, not frightened but on guard, as a boy will look when he expects some demand to be made of him which he is not sure how to meet.

Magda walked up between the chairs, curtseyed to the boy, and stood beside the chairman.

"This is a matter," she began, "in which we have all

pledged our lives and all we possess. In so great a cause we shall not grudge them. Let us therefore make quite certain, before we go any further, of the foundations upon which we build. Mr. Chairman, with great boldness and great respect I beg your leave to ask one or two questions."

"Continue, *gnädiges* Fräulein."

"First. We all heard with deep regret, at the time of the fall of Berlin, that the Reichsleiter Martin Bormann was among the slain. Will our gracious and distinguished visitor be so good as to tell us what we are to answer when we are asked: 'How do you know that this is the same man?'"

She drew back, leaning against the wall, and Martin Bormann rose to his feet.

"I am glad that that question has been asked and I thank the Fräulein von Bergen for asking it. To reply, I must take you back to the tragic days of the fearful *Götterdämmerung* which befell us in April 1945.

"I was, as you know, in the bunker of the Reich Chancellery with our beloved Führer and his few faithful followers. I spent most of the time in keeping a close record of every event, hour by hour, of those fateful days, noting down as far as possible verbatim not only every word which was spoken by our beloved Führer but everything which was said by any of those present. History will require my record, future generations will demand it. I take it with me wherever I go, I have it with me here.

"In the last days—on April the twenty-eighth, to be exact —my Führer called me into his room and ordered me, upon my obedience, to do my utmost to escape alive. He laid it upon me as a duty. Not only me, in point of fact, but all those present except one——" He hesitated, glanced at the boy, and went on: "Our task was to rebuild the National Socialist state. Only Dr. Goebbels refused to obey; he and his wife and their six young children died there.

"Very unwillingly, for it would have been so much easier to die, I promised. April the twenty-ninth. I signed the marriage certificate and witnessed both the Führer's private will and his political testament. April the thirtieth. He—they died. I stood by the trench in which their bodies lay. I watched the leaping flames.

"Late in the evening of the following day, at about twenty-two hours, those of us who were left alive began the attempt to obey our Führer's last order, to escape. We divided into several small groups and went out at short intervals. We went out into the Wilhelmstrasse, down into the Underground, and along to the Friedrichstrasse with the idea of crossing the Weidendamm Bridge. We had heard that it was not actually held by the Russians, though they had it under heavy fire.

"I can't describe to you what it was like passing along the Friedrichstrasse. It was fantastic, it was so appalling that it passed belief and became unreal. Everywhere houses were blazing furiously, the scene was as light as day, there were flames everywhere, the crash of bursting shells mingled with the crash of falling houses and the continual rattle of small-arms fire. It was impossible for a group to keep together, though I am told that the first one did. I can't imagine how they managed it. They got across the Weidendamm Bridge, but the shelling was so heavy that they had to take refuge in a cellar, where they were all captured by the Russians.

"Obersturmbannführer Erich Kempka, who was the officer in charge of the Motors Pool at the Reich Chancellery, came up with a German tank. It was driven slowly along the street and we all walked beside it; it protected us on one side at least. If you can imagine how naked we felt! We reached the bridge. State Secretary Naumann of the Propaganda Ministry, the Führer's personal physician Dr. Ludwig Stumpfegger, and I walked on the left side of the tank while Kempka and another man named Rattenhuber walked on the right. We were almost across the bridge when the tank was hit by a *Panzerfaust* which exploded inside and blew out the left side of the tank—my side. That's where I got this," said Bormann, lifting his chin and touching the scar on his neck. "I fell down and rolled away and crawled off the bridge. I tied my handkerchief round my neck and a scarf tightly over it. I was in frightful pain. I crawled, with pauses, for a long way. Every time a Russian soldier came near me I shammed dead. Presently, when I had convinced myself that my jugular vein was not severed"—he smiled—"I staggered to my feet.

"You will not expect me to tell you the names of those who bound my wounds, fed me, sheltered me, and passed me on to others. Indeed, in some cases I do not even know their names. I was making for Hamburg to meet Grand Admiral Doenitz, but he was a prisoner long before I reached there.

"I should detain you all night and weary you to death if I told the full story of how I got out of the country and eventually reached Spain. There I found peace and shelter and time, which heals all wounds, even worse ones than this," and again he touched his neck. "By degrees I regained enough strength and energy to take up the task which my Führer set me, that of rebuilding the National Socialist state. In your eager faces now before me, I see the first early blades of the great harvest that shall follow."

Martin Bormann finished his statement and waited for the applause to die down. Then he turned towards Magda, still standing against the wall behind him, and said kindly: "Well? Are you satisfied, *gnädiges* Fräulein, that I am the Herr Reichsleiter Martin Bormann?"

Magda took a step forward. "I am satisfied," she said clearly, and the applause broke out again.

"Have you another question, Fräulein?" asked the chairman.

"If it please you and this meeting," said Magda. "I must first explain that my father, the Herr Doktor August-Wilhelm von Bergen, surgeon, was in practice at Munich from 1922 till 1943, when he retired to live here, at Cologne. He was very successful, greatly respected, and much esteemed in particular for his treatment of women and children. He was, therefore, one of those called in when a child was born in 1935 of the lady Eva Braun."

There was a distinct stir in the room, and the boy, who had been fidgeting with a complicated pocketknife with numerous fittings, turned his head sharply and looked up at the speaker. As for the listener outside the window, it was as well that none molested him, for he would not have observed a squadron of cavalry charging towards him, so completely absorbed he was.

"We all know," went on Magda, "that for the past five years he whom we all revere as *Die Hoffnung*"—that is, The Hope—"has been moved about from place to place, transferred from the loving care of one person to the warm affection of another again and again, has gone under different names and been taught to tell various stories of his parentage and upbringing to accord with the background of the moment. What a life for a child," said Magda in tones of pity, and a murmur ran round the room while the boy turned scarlet to the hair and hung his head. "Among some of my father's papers which I only examined recently, I found this. Herr President, perhaps you will tell the meeting what it is."

She gave the paper to the chairman, who unfolded it, stared, glanced at Magda, and looked at the paper again. It was headed with the official stamp of the Third Reich, and the chairman, in a trembling voice, said so. "Underneath is written: 'The fingerprints of Siegfried Adolf, aged six weeks.' Beneath that again, gentlemen, ten tiny fingerprints taken in the official manner. Below that again a set of signatures of which the first is A. Hitler. There follow those of Eva Braun, Martin Bormann"—with a bow to Bormann—"Dr. J. Goebbels, Dr. August-Wilhelm von Bergen, and another name I do not recognize."

Bormann leaned forward, smiling. "The last is the signature of the chief of police for the city of Munich, under whose expert direction these prints were taken. I may add that the subject loudly resented the proceedings," he added, and a laugh went round the room while the boy blushed more hotly than ever and wound his feet round the legs of his chair.

"I should suppose," continued Magda, "that there were a number of copies of that document—that itself is a replica, as you see—but it occurred to me that perhaps this might be the only one which survived the disruption of our archives. In that case, and having regard to the secrecy in which Die Hoffnung has been hidden, I thought it might prove useful in case his identity were ever called in question at any——"

Her sentence was cut off by a burst of applause led by the chairman; Martin Bormann rose to his feet and Magda stepped modestly back.

"I shall say first," said Bormann, "and I will tolerate no contradiction, that if the Fräulein Magda von Bergen is a fair sample of the youth of our party, I have more faith in its future than I ever——" But again cheering drowned the end of the sentence, until he held up his hand for silence. "Each of the signatories to that document had a copy," he continued. "I had. Mine was destroyed during my wanderings; heaven knows what became of the others. Only the other day I thought of these certificates and despaired of ever finding one. Now, like a gift from the gods, one falls into our hands at the best——"

He continued to rejoice while Hambledon, outside the window, put both hands to his head and rubbed it tenderly.

"What the devil's the girl playing at? She told me she was going to smash up the party, and here she is—— If she's double-crossing me I'll——"

Magda's voice broke in on his painful thoughts and there was something in its tone which rang a warning in his ear.

"There is one more paper which was put away with the fingerprint certificate; here it is. Perhaps the Herr President will be so good as to read out this also."

"This paper," said the chairman willingly, "is headed 'Munich, April 17, 1943,' and continues, 'I, August-Wilhelm von Bergen, surgeon, do solemnly declare that in May 1936 I operated upon Siegfried Adolf, son of Eva Braun, for hernia; that after that year I did not see him again until today, when I was directed to conduct a thorough general examination to ascertain the cause of some digestive trouble from which he suffered. I do solemnly swear that the boy I examined today had no hernia-operation scar—and—therefore"—the chairman's voice faltered, but he seemed unable to stop reading aloud—" 'it cannot be—the—same—boy . . .'" His voice tailed off into silence.

"*What?*" shrieked the boy, and there was a loud and confused babble of sound penetrated by Bormann's voice shouting for silence.

"I'll have her knighted," said Hambledon outside, inaudibly thumping the stone window sill, "I'll buy her a diamond necklace, I'll marry her to a duke, dammit, I'll marry her myself——"

"Silence!" roared Bormann, and the uproar stopped as though switched off. "This is a lie; the old man was in his dotage. My dear boy——"

"There is a simple way to prove it," said Magda, pointing to the certificate. "The fingerprints. I see Herr Paul Koenen here; he is, I believe, a fingerprint expert of the police——"

"The devil he is," said Hambledon.

"Let him take the fingerprints of our beloved, *Die Hoff-*

*nung*, and settle this business once for all," cried Magda. "Myself, I do not believe it."

Bormann was on his feet, shouting that he would not permit it, it was an insult to *Die Hoffnung*, the suggestion should never have been made. Swollen by conceit and a few kind words, the woman Von Bergen had blasphemed their glory and disgraced herself. Let her be destroyed at once as a poisoner of men's minds and a——

More uproar interrupted him, shouts of "The fingerprints!" and "The vote, put it to the vote!" The chairman hammered on the table for order and did not get it until, with a sudden gauche movement, the dark-haired boy sprang to his feet and spoke in the half-broken voice of his age, alternately deep and shrill, under the circumstances infinitely moving. Magda von Bergen clapped her hand over her mouth and her eyes filled with tears.

"Herr President. As the person most concerned, I say that this matter must be settled. It would be impossible to live with such a doubt always at the back of—always present in my mind. You must know, I must know. Let my fingerprints be taken."

"No," said Bormann stubbornly. "I will not allow it."

"*Why not?*"

"My dear boy, you don't understand——"

The boy turned to the chairman. "Let Herr Koenen come forward."

The chairman wrung his hands. "This is dreadful. This is all most irregular. Order! Order! I will have order. Action of this nature cannot be taken without a motion properly proposed and seconded, and a vote——"

"That's simple," said the boy, turning towards the meeting with one hand held high. "Those in favour?"

"Oh God," said Hambledon, outside, "I like this boy. Oh dear, this is——"

"Carried by a large majority," said the boy triumphantly, and added with a nervous giggle: "Come on, Herr Koenen. Do your stuff!"

Magda von Bergen slipped from behind the table and fled back to her seat, weeping. Paul Koenen rose and said that he had no ink with him suitable for the purpose.

"Find something else, then," said Siegfried Adolf reasonably. "Lampblack. Soot. Whatever the woman here cleaned my shoes with this morning."

One of the members slipped out at the door, and Bormann said that if *Die Hoffnung* insisted, of course the farce should be carried through, but it was only a farce. The baby prints on the certificate had probably been forged.

"You acknowledged them just now," said the chairman justly.

"I didn't examine them," argued Bormann. "I shouldn't be any the wiser if I did; what do I know about fingerprints? But I do know a plot when I see one, and this is a plot to discredit you, our Hope. That woman——"

"You know," said the boy, leaning his hands on the table and looking intently at Bormann, "you know, anybody'd think you *knew* they weren't going to match."

There followed a period of utter silence unbroken till the door opened and the messenger came back with a tray in his hands upon which was an assortment of tins: black enamel paint, stove polish, black shoe polish, a piece of charcoal, and a tin lid with some soot in it. Paul Koenen, with obvious reluctance, took the tray from him and walked up to the table.

"Well, you ought to get something out of that lot," said Siegfried Adolf. "Which are you going to use?"

Koenen tried one or two with his own fingers; the shoe polish gave the best result. Hambledon could bear no longer the agony of hearing and not seeing; judging correctly that everyone would be watching intently what was going on at the table, he drew a pencil from his pocket, slipped his hand through the half-open shutter, and gently pushed the curtain aside. He saw a narrow section of the group at the table; not Bormann, who was beyond his view, but the left-hand half of the chairman, a side view of Koenen bending over a tray, and a full view of a white-faced boy with a heavy lock of dark hair falling over his forehead.

"This one, I think," said Koenen. There was a thick glass ash tray on the table; he turned it upside down, disclosing a flat surface which he smeared with shoe polish, spreading and rubbing it over until it was thin and smooth and reasonably even. "This is a very unprofessional method," he said, "but I think it will do." He straightened himself. "Now, if you're ready——"

The boy stood motionless for a second and then jerked away, hiding his hands behind his back. Hambledon caught his breath, and at that precise moment a hand fell upon his shoulder.

He started so violently that he all but dropped the pencil and the shutter rattled a little.

"Sorry I startled you," whispered the officer in command of the troops. "We're all round the house and all the windows are open—simple."

"Be quiet or I'll kill you," muttered Hambledon fiercely. "Wait!"

He rearranged his curtain and looked again. The boy, biting his lip, was very carefully rolling his fingers on the black surface and then pressing them on a sheet of paper, with Koenen giving directions in a low voice.

"Thank you," he said at last, and the boy drew back, wiping his fingers on his handkerchief while Koenen looked from one set of prints to the other. Then he stood up, drew a spectacle case out of his pocket, took out the spectacles, settled them on his nose, and looked again. There was not a sound in the room, not even the faint sound of breathing.

Koenen shook his head.

"Aren't they the same?" asked Siegfried Adolf, and his voice had gone squeaky.

"They——" Koenen tried to clear his throat and failed. "They are not even the same type," he croaked.

There was a sighing sound in the room, as though everyone let out his breath at once, and then the silence was broken by the boy.

"This is your doing!" he shouted at Bormann. "You've cheated me. I'm not real, I'm a fraud—you did it, you beast——"

"Now," said Hambledon, drawing back from the window. "Carry on, it's all over."

There came the shrill blast of a whistle close to his ear, thrilling, deafening, then shouting and the crash of shutters flung back as the soldiers leaped into the room, and instantly the lights went out. Inside the room somebody fired a shot, then another and another and half a dozen more, while somewhere at the back of the house a woman screamed twice and then stopped.

The officer bellowed an order to stop that shooting and switch on the lights, men thrust past Hambledon this way and that, and there was an indeterminate struggle round the door.

Hambledon awoke to sudden life. "Bormann," he shouted, "that fellow by the table, take him at all costs," and he scrambled through the window, switching on his torch, which showed him a scene like a disorganized Rugby scrum complicated by fallen chairs, and the uproar was deafening till somebody switched on the lights, when it died down suddenly and ceased.

The officer bellowed that everyone was his prisoner. "Put your hands up!" Hambledon forced his way through, looking for Bormann, and at last reached the table.

The chairman stood there, holding his hands above his head, with his gold-rimmed spectacles still on his nose and his dignity only marred by the fact that his waistcoat was ripped from top to bottom.

In front of the table Magda von Bergen was kneeling, sobbing bitterly, with the boy's head on her lap. He was lying quite still, sprawled upon the floor; Hambledon bent over him and lifted his head. One of the bullets fired at random in the dark had struck him in the left temple and killed him instantly.

Martin Bormann was nowhere to be seen.


The Cologne–Paris express pulled out of the frontier station at Jeumont and rolled on into France; D'Almeida and Piccione leaned back in their seats and sighed their relief.

"The last hurdle successfully cleared," said Hambledon, who had been watching them.

"That is so, Señor Hambledon. At the Spanish frontier there will be no trouble; we can deal with the Spanish frontier. There, we are at home. But to carry all that money through the customs at Aachen, Herbesthal, Erquelinnes, and again at Jeumont without its being discovered, it is to shorten the life. When that Belgian Currency Control officer looked so hard at me just now I wished with all my heart that it was still in the safe of the Dom Hotel."

"You looked so innocent," said Forgan, "that if I had been in his place I should have suspected you at once."

"Instead of which they all suspected me," said Yeoman gloomily. "One would have thought that I was a notorious dope smuggler."

"Not dope," said Tommy Hambledon, "diamonds. When that feller levered off the heels of your best brown shoes with a screw driver I thought you were going to punch his nose."

"If Magda hadn't been with me I would have done so," said Yeoman. "They will never be the same again."

"Oh, nonsense," said Tommy. "An honest English cobbler will make them as good as ever. I wonder how you will like England, Fräulein."

Magda turned her abstracted gaze from the window to Hambledon's face and said: "I beg your pardon, you spoke to me?"

"Cheer up," said Hambledon. "Things are best as they are, when you come to think about what might have happened otherwise. That Silver Ghosts business couldn't have been allowed to succeed, you know."

"No, I know," said Magda. "It isn't the Silver Ghosts which lie on my conscience, it is——"

"Darling, don't fret so," said Yeoman. "You didn't shoot him."

"No, but I started all the trouble."

"Listen, Fräulein," said Hambledon. "If you hadn't done so, I should. I am a fair shot with an automatic, and that performance had got to be *stopped*."

"But," said Forgan, looking at the grim face next him, "surely you would have shot Bormann?"

"From where I stood," said Hambledon quietly, "I couldn't see Bormann."

"Oh dear," said Forgan under his breath.

"Fräulein," said Hambledon to Magda, who, owing to the noise of the train, had not heard his last remark, "Fräulein Magda, you have now a chance to start a new life and be happy. Do not throw it all away by brooding over what can't be helped. There was no future in this life for that poor boy; so long as he lived he would have been a source of trouble. You know that's true." She nodded unwillingly. "Put it all out of your mind and look to the future."

"Talking about Bormann," said D'Almeida with ready tact, "I shall always wonder how he got away."

"Slipped out in the confusion and climbed a tree, of course," said Campbell, " 'while far below the Roundhead rode and hummed a surly hymn.' "

"There he sat," said Forgan, "suffering from nothing worse than pins and needles and spiders down the neck until the soldiers gave up looking for him and went away. Then he slid down the tree trunk and repaired to the Schloss Rensburg, where the Baroness Hildegarde hid him in her wardrobe."

"Feeding him, as and when possible, on chicken drumsticks and cold potatoes smuggled away in her napkin from the castle dinner table," said Campbell. "When it was too long between meals he chewed her riding boots."

"You know," said Magda, "I've been thinking about that. He must have begun his escape before the shooting started; the lights went on so soon."

"Oh yes," said Hambledon. "He didn't wait for anything or anybody. He's harmless now; his name's mud in Germany from now on forever. He tried to fool you all and then ran away."

"Will he come back to Spain, do you think?" said D'Almeida.

"I'm prepared to bet that he'll be there before you," said Campbell. "What that bird doesn't know about crossing frontiers isn't worth knowing."

"Then I think I will see if a little mud cannot be attached to him in Spain also," said D'Almeida.

"By the time you've done with him," said Forgan, "he'll be glad to emigrate to Buenos Aires, even on a cargo boat."

D'Almeida shuddered exaggeratedly. "By the way," he said, "that reminds me. You are still wearing our clothes."

"You shall have them back in Paris," said Forgan handsomely. "Our luggage has been parked at the Gare du Nord all this time; we'll get it out and resume our proper habiliments. These are nice suits, but they're too tight in the sleeves."

"Then, when we're all ourselves again," said Campbell, "we'll start out and really show you Paris."

"Yes, why not?" said Forgan. "You've got all your travellers' cheques intact, we didn't touch them."

"Thank you," said Piccione with emphasis. "I think not."

"Come to Spain," urged D'Almeida, "come and stay with me and we will show you Madrid."

"May we bring Spelmann to find us if we get lost?"

"What's happened to Herr Spelmann?" asked Magda.

"Oh, he's all right," said Hambledon. "He's landed a job with the Security people at Bonn. It's nice to think that we left one completely happy man behind us; I saw him crossing the square yesterday and a policeman saluted him."

"So our time in Germany was not entirely wasted," said Forgan.

"Of course not," said D'Almeida. "Also, you taught us to play poker."